Relay-tionships

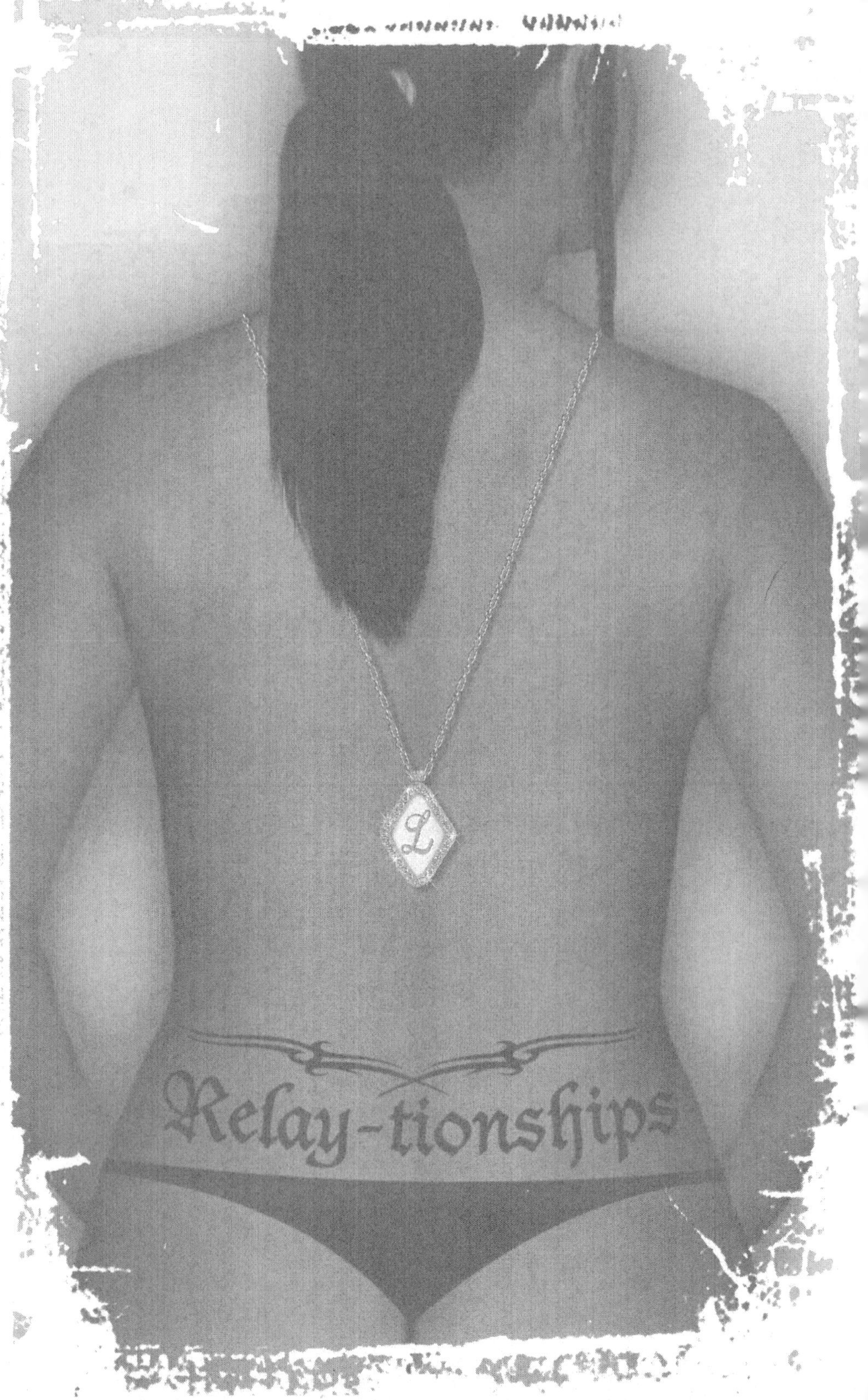
L
Relay-tionships

Relay-tionships

Andreia Solomon Burke

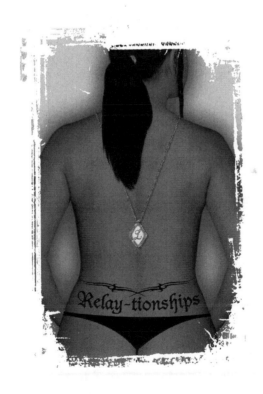

Published by
L.A. Press

© 2009 L.A. Press

Published by L.A. Press

Cover Concept: Lloyd S. Burke
Book Cover design: Lee 'leebs' Baker
leebs69@hotmail.com
Photography: Jerry Sweet
Editor: Frances F. Ford
Editor: Kelvin Harewood

www.myspace.com/msrelaytionships

ISBN: 978-0-9561946-0-2

Relay-tionships

About the Author

New author, Andreia Solomon Burke was born on July 30th 1964 in Brooklyn, New York. After the death of her mother, Andreia moved to Charlotte, N.C where she attended college. Her final move within the U.S. was to Atlanta, GA. Andreia and her husband have two beautiful daughters, Le'Dreia and Alexus. Andreia is most proud of her title as grandmother to her only grandson, I'Santi. Andreia currently lives in London, England with her husband Lloyd of twenty-one years and their youngest daughter Alexus.

Relay-tionships

My Dedications

To my Husband Burkie, I've always called you the strongest man I know and that haven't changed. You have always been one of my biggest supporters and this book is dedicated to you. If I had not taken this journey with you, there wouldn't be a book and for that I am forever grateful!! Thanks for all of your support emotionally and financially. I love you!

To Grandma's baby boy Santi, there aren't enough words and not enough time to tell you how much I love you. From the first day I looked at you, I was in love. You bring me so much joy just by looking at you. We will be together again soon and we will do everything we want to do!! Keep on protecting your mommy. I love you Santi.

To Le'Dreia my first born, it is because of you I live. You know that you saved my life and are the reason I learned how to love and be a better woman. I have always admired your strength and courage. You have made me so proud and I know your grandma is equally as proud; may she rest in peace.

To my nephew E.J,I love you so very much! I thank God that HE put us back together. Remember what I told you… the world is yours. (I.S.G.T.M.S)

To my star Alexus, I didn't know it was possible to love someone as much as I love you! You're my Special angel. You have blossomed into such a wonderful human being and God is about to bless you tremendously. Keep reaching for the sky, you're already a star!!!!!!!!!

To my only brother Ed, I know we both have spouses and children, but you know; I feel like we're in the world all by ourselves. We have been through so much together. I love you so much. You'll always stand to be the best brother in the world. Thanks for all you do! And like mommy use to always tell us," …that what doesn't kill us" you know the rest. (Where's my money Ramel) I love you Ty and Brooklyn.

To my sister Von, you know what you mean to me. I love you so much. You are the strongest woman I know. No one has endured as much as you and can still love life the way you do. You have taught me so much. I just want you to be happy!!!

Relay-tionships

Acknowledgements

"As for you, you meant evil against me, but God meant it for good in order to bring about this present change...Gen 50.20

I give all praises to God, I could not even imagine the plans He had for me and my family, and I thank Him for it. Now to the people whom I love and respect, it is my pleasure to thank and acknowledge you here.

Pop, I know we've had our rough patches in the past, but I have always been thankful to you for instilling in me the pride of hard work, but most of all I love you for loving my children so much.

Auntie and Uncle Howard, I love you so very much. Thank you for always being there for me. Before mommie was gone and especially after.

Uncle Roger, what can I say...you mean the world to me. I love you so much. Your integrity is astounding. Thank you for always taking pride in your family. I love you Aunt Barbara.

Aunt Bootee, I thank you and Uncle Bobby for caring for Lou at the time I needed you two the most. I won't ever forget it. I love you.

Frances" Mama" Ford. I want to thank you for all your words of encouragement that got me through the rough days. All I had to do is look on my wall and read your prayers. Thank you for saying "yes" without hesitation to be the editor for my book.

Jermaine Holley, you're the best! I am so proud of you and what you are to me. Your inspirational words have carried me even while I'm over here. Keep writing and encouraging.

Lance Holder, you are my dawg. When you came into my life; I knew then without a doubt that God places people in your life for a purpose. So many days I wanted to give up, but your ears and sense of humour kept me going. Peace to you and your family.

Judy Baker, there aren't enough words to express the gratitude I have for you. You have helped me and my family tremendously when I couldn't call on anyone else. For that I'll always love you!

Joe Duggan, you inspired me so much the first day I met you at the Streatham poetry club. You may have forgotten but I told you then, I felt your spirit that night and I was right. You are a wonderful human being.

leebs, thank you for working with me on my first project. I know we will have a long lasting relationship. You're a genius! See you on my next project!

Alex Wheatle, when I read your book "The Dirty South" it did a marvellous thing for me; I picked up my pen and started writing again. Thank you for all your advice and help. I can't wait to see "Brixton Rock "in the cinemas.

Robert Beckford, thank you for introducing me to; two of the most fascinating bars in London. I thank you from the depths of my heart for all you have done for me. You continue to be an inspiration.

Kelvin Harewood, I appreciate you taking on this project so late in the game. Your contribution to my book was tremendous! Thank you!

All my CHRIS Kids and Beginners Poetry family I love you!

All my family and extended family that I didn't mention in print, please know in my heart I appreciate and love all of you.

Prologue

I wondered who Dre was talking to as I watched him in secret. His eyes sparkled the entire time he talked on the phone. The sparkle seemed familiar, as that was the same sparkle we once shared...but no more. Lately all I got were cold touches and dead stares. Maybe we did get too close, too soon, after Greg. I had hoped Dre was the breath of fresh air I needed after dealing with Greg and his shenanigans. Even with all the shit that Greg put me through, there was something about him that made me drop everything and run to his side when he called. Dre kept warning me that he wouldn't stand for my need to be Greg's crutch too much longer.

Maybe I should have listened to Dre's threats which proved to be promises. Dre's words kept assuring me that he wasn't cheating, but his eyes were telling a different story. What did he want from me?, I thought if no one else, Dre would understand what I'd been going through. With my mother's health failing rapidly, me and my unexplained weight gain which I couldn't seem to shed, no matter what I did. And then there were times that Greg legitimately needed my help. I thought for sure Dre would be sympathetic.

These days Dre found fault in everything I did. Dre even complained about me spending too much time helping my girl Charmine. Her wedding was coming up and I was not only her best friend; I was her maid of honour. I'm an only child, so it is so nice having a friend like Charmine; she was more like my sister. We shared everything, the good, the bad and the ugly...well I can't say everything. Our taste in men was like night and day. Charmine loves the men in suit types, clean shaven and who talked about politics, but me; I lose control over the dark chocolate brotha who had that thug swagger that exuded confidence. It didn't matter if he wore Stacey Adams...Timbs are just fine. However, I did require that he had a sense of direction and brought more than just his dick into the relationship.

The closer we got to Charmine's wedding, the more Dre complained. At nights I saw less and less of him. There were some nights he didn't even come home, but I chalked it up to him needing to spend time with his boys. I discovered later I couldn't have been more wrong. The day of Charmine's wedding, she looked as through six angels had dressed her in her strapless Vera Wang gown. With her make-up professionally done, Charmine looked absolutely flawless. As I clasped the diamond necklace that Kamel had given her as a pre-wedding gift around her neck, she grabbed my hand and said her stomach was doing flips. I tried calming her down by assuring her it was just the wedding day jitters and poured her a glass of wine. After a few sips, the wine seemed to help.

Charmine and I sat on the red satin, padded bench in the dressing room and laughed about the twists and turns our lives had taken thus far. Charmine and I were laughing so loudly, that when I heard the door open, I thought it was an usher telling us to hush. Instead it was Mrs Grant, Charmine's mother. She walked in the room avoiding our eyes, but I could tell she had been crying. Charmine jumped up thinking her mother's appearance was her cue for show time. However, what Mrs Grant had hit us with was no laughing matter. She passed a crumbled note to her daughter, which was on the back of a soiled food menu. Mrs Grant squeaked out to Charmine that Kamel had given the note to an usher to give to her. Charmine took the note from her mother's clutches and began to read silently. I watched my best friend's chest heave in and out as if she was gasping for her life.

I did not have to read the note to know what was happening. I watched as Charmine ripped the diamond necklace from her throat and collapse to the floor. I rushed to my sis-tah's side, while Mrs Grant ran into the sanctuary to get her husband. My unanswered cell phone rang fervently while I was on the floor consoling my friend. I was so relieved to see Mr Grant enter the room. I was hoping that he would be able to get Charmine to come around, something I was unable to do, ever since her mother left the room.

Before I could even check to see who'd been calling me like there was a fire in my house, my phone rings again. I answered hoping that it was Kamel with an explanation for his behaviour. Listening to the sultry voice on the other end, it was apparent it wasn't Kamel. Instead it would have to be Dre who would need to explain to me why a woman named Renee was calling demanding to speak to me about her and Dre.

Chapter One

As I lie impatiently on the table in the Dial Sun Nail salon, I wished that Ling would hurry up and finish waxing my eyebrows. I still had a lot more to do before my evening out with Clay. I hoped that tonight, stripped of my inhibitions, he would see that I loved him. Yet, make him understand I need to move back home. My mother needs me and I felt I'd already let her down enough and I couldn't continue to ignore that fact. I just wanted to make him see that my move had absolutely nothing to do with Dre.

A few thoughts and minutes later, Ling gently taps my shoulder; her signal to indicate she is finished. "All done" Ling says, as she gives me a hand mirror to admire her work. I took the mirror and inspected my eyebrows because everything had to be perfect tonight. I smiled and returned Ling's mirror. I paid Ling her fee, with a tip, as she outdid herself today. "Thanks Ling" I said, as I steal one last glimpse of myself and left her shop. Ling waves and sends me off with her usual, "See you next week" pitch.

As I headed towards my baby, my astral black GS 300 Lexus,

I debated… should I get her waxed today or wait until tomorrow when I have more time? I quickly glanced at my watch and thought one more day wouldn't hurt; she'll understand. I took my coat off before entering my car; it was rather warm for a winter's day. To be honest, the weather was one of the pros in helping me make my decision to move south when I was planning to re-locate from Brooklyn. However, I did miss New York at Christmas time; there was no place like Rockefeller Center and the smell of roasted chestnuts while walking in Manhattan, but I knew I would have lost my mind if I stayed.

As I listened to Mercedes on V-103, I went back to the last day I spent in New York. Char and I were packing the last few boxes while waiting for the moving company to load the rest of my belongings and end my chapter in Brooklyn. Char told me to grab the tape from the kitchen so that she could secure the last box of books. I headed for the kitchen and there he stood, just the sight of him left me immobile. At my hall closet door, I came to a full halt; stunned by his presence.

"Dre what the fuck are you doing here?" Shit, I forgot to get his key in my haste to throw his shit, and his ass out of the house, I recanted.

"I had to come Lane; I had to see if you was really leaving or was it all a bad dream?" Dre asked me as he is walking closer to me.

"Yes, I'm leaving and no it's not a dream; this is for fucking real!"

"Lane" Dre continues, "I'm sorry, I"… I stopped him from coming any closer, I threw up my hand to create a flimsy barrier. I didn't allow him to finish his sentence. "Yeah Dre, about as sorry as you was while fucking that broad in our home!" Dre just stood there trying to look pitiful.

"Just go!" I managed to squeak out without collapsing. Char

walked out of the bedroom to inquire about what was the holdup with the tape. She hadn't yet realized we had an unwanted intruder until her eyes followed my horrid glare. She spotted Dre and her voice raised three octaves, "What the fuck are you doing here?" Char looked at me as if I had the answer. When she realized the blank stare that has riddled my face, she continued to direct all of her anger and questions back at Dre. "Haven't you caused enough trouble? Get the hell out of here!"

I didn't even notice if he had left or not because I took off for my bedroom like a bat out of hell, because at any moment I thought my legs were going to give way. As fast as Char was in the room behind me, I knew she did not see him out either. I fell backwards and slid down against the newly bare wall; as if all my bones had caved in. Char grabbed both of my hands and met me on the floor. Through my tears, I looked at Char and threw myself in her bosom; at that very moment I truly knew what best friends and sisterhood is all about. I had never had such a connection with a woman, other than my mother as I did with Char. We met in college and we've been joined at the hip since. We both graduated top of our class; I got my Masters in finance when not that many sis-tahs were getting degrees in finance and accounting. It was considered a man's field but I loved the numbers game so it was natural for me.

Char received her law degree and was approached by several firms before she could even hang her degree on her wall. We have always been so supportive of each other. So much so that she joined me in Atlanta the same year Dre had me almost suicidal. When I felt my bones strengthen again, I made my move to head for the kitchen to get some juice for the both of us. I was so depleted from the whole Dre episode. He knew he always had that effect on me and that is why he decided to come today. He always relied on the fact that he was fine, coupled with a banging body; I would give him a pass as I had done so many times before. Dre had me so shook; I was creeping in my own house thinking he would spring out from anywhere. Good. No sign of him I proclaimed, as I approached the fridge and there it was; Dre's last feeble attempt to send me batty. I took the note he left from the fridge and handled it like dynamite about to detonate.

Lane,

I don't know what to say, but please forgive me. I never meant to hurt you. You are; and will always be the love of my life. To think about how I fucked up pains me, because I know you did not deserve that. I love you Lane, please make me whole again, say you want me and I promise I will cherish you, as you should have been from the day you allowed me in your life. You always said how much you loved and admired me because I am so strong... but I'm not Lane, I feel weak without you, I need you. I love you baby.

DRE

My body quivered as I re-lived that day, with his words still in my head. I shook it off and said aloud, "Yeah you did fuck up, and I will never allow myself to get that low again." I turned up the volume to tune in to Mercedes; to hear what guests she would be celebrating her return to V-103 with. I knew she was a true testament of how you recover from a fuck up and it gave me hope towards my own recovery, and it didn't hurt that Clay was also helping me with my progress. I headed towards Phelps Plaza to complete what I considered the most important night I had in a long time. I knew it was all about us and nothing could go wrong. Traffic was crazy as I approached the interstate, but what did I expect, it's a beautiful Friday and I doubt if I'm the only one with plans. Mentally preparing myself for the traffic, I put in one of my favorite CDs; my girl MJB, if anybody could take your mind off bullshit, it was her.

I was about to sulk that I couldn't fit a fucking thing off Victoria Secret's rack, which was going to cause me extra travel time to the voluptuous girl shop but I quickly perked up knowing how much he loved my curves, and I mean every inch. With my girls being a size eight or smaller, I was the thickest one in my circle. True, I had ass and tits, but at least I knew Clay did not use me as eye candy because he felt insecure. Not like Char's ex-fiancé Kamel, he used to tell her, "Gain an ounce, you gotta bounce!" He was so the total opposite of Clay.

Now like I said, I'm the thickest of my girls; but I am fine! I have to admit I take pride in the fact that women envy my cleavage and my lady humps, but it was my eyes and lips that seemed to drive the men crazy. When I met a man for the first time they stared into my eyes as if they were mesmerized, and the way they searched my lips and mouth was like they were envisioning me sucking their dick right where we stood. Even after a few dates with Clay, he admitted that my lips caused him to have erotic dreams about us. He always complimented me on my lips, especially when I wore my Fashion Fair Sheerly Clear; so I always made sure I had an ample supply of it. As the last song played on my CD, I was making the turn into Phelps Plaza.

I drove around for a few minutes looking for a parking space, which was never an easy feat. I continued to look around hoping I could park as close to the entrance as possible, but I knew I was asking too much. Still in search of a parking space, I made myself a vow to get in and out. I need that negligee that yells "fuck me", followed by a quick trip into Bath and Body and home I go. I still had some minor preparations I had to take care of before meeting Clay at eight. I wondered where he would be taking me even though it really didn't matter. I was just happy to be in the same room with him, put it like this; the way I loved Clay, I was overjoyed that we were living at the same time. I almost felt like I couldn't live without him which was a scary thought for two reasons. One, I'd been down this road before and two, we're at the very early stage of our relationship and although I knew he enjoyed being with me, I couldn't answer one hundred percent to where his head was at. I entered the lingerie boutique and was half-ass greeted by a sales associate that clearly did not want to be at work.

"Can I help you?", the young lady with bad teeth and attitude asks.

"No, I'm good." I respond. Not even looking her way, I head straight to where I can see heaven on satin hangers. I looked at several before picking up the one that met all the criteria. Yes it was black, yes it was sheer, yes it would accentuate all my curves, and most importantly; it yelled, "FUCK ME!" I found a full length mirror and held it in front of me; I just didn't have the time to try it on in the boutique so I took a mental photo, smiled and walked my purchase to the check out. The sales associate behind the counter was much more pleasant, "Hmm," she jests, "Someone has a special night planned." Her statement brought an involuntary smile to my face. "I hope it will be." I'm now in a full blown giddiness. "Can you tell me who helped you?"

"No one", I answered feeling slightly guilty; I wondered if I should have lied, so the young lady who greeted me could at least have claimed the commission. I'm fully aware that commission is a huge part of their wages, but I thought against it, as I felt I would be doing fellow customers an injustice if I lied. She just needs to get her game up.

"Alright then, is this all?"

"Yes, for now." I replied and gave her my credit card and ID. She says "thanks" as she takes my payment with a broad grin. A minute or two later and my transaction is complete. "Have a great night, and come again.", the pleasant salesperson grinned at me.

"I will, and thanks."

I exited the boutique trying to remember which end I'm on for the quickest route to Bath and Body shop. I took the escalator downstairs and got lucky as the shop is staring me in my face. I'm going to be on time after all I thought. I inhaled the entire splendor of aromatherapy entering the doors of B&B. I grabbed my favorite scents and got the hell out of Dodge. I left the mall in record time for me; and I'm proud of myself. Now if I could only do to the same with this traffic. I knew I would be wishing for the impossible, it was already after four o'clock; in addition to it being Friday. I had to make the grueling decision, do I take the streets or the interstate? I go back and forth with this until I forced myself to just pick one, alright the interstate it is.

Once I exited the mall I spent nearly twenty minutes trying to locate my baby. I hate when I do this, I forgot the parking row number, and why is it that when you try to locate your car, everyone appears to have the same color car as you. How ridiculous this is. I'm losing the time I saved in the mall looking for my car. I walked over two more rows and there she is. Now I'm cooking with oil, I just remembered that yellow mustang with the Florida plates; thank God it was still parked here.

I disarm the system, jump in and now I can head home. I thought about my purchases and thought about the night, with what I had in store for Clay how could I go wrong? I can't! As I approached the snail-like pace of I-85, I relished in the memory of how Clay and I met and how I almost let my past relationship with Dre interfere with my future happiness. I'm so glad he never gave up on me and gave us a second chance.

Chapter Two

I met Clay at a time in my life when I wasn't even looking for love. I was at a point, I was happy with myself. I had a great job, great friends and family; plus I traveled whenever and wherever I wanted. The night we met it was a girls night out, Char had tickets to a Hawks vs. Knicks game at Phillips. Char knew I would be game because I still repped New York to the fullest. Char also knew I hated extreme cold weather so the night of the game she nervously kept calling my house. I'd brought some work home which I needed to finish before going to the game, so each time she called I let it go to voicemail. Char must have translated the non-responding to her calls as if I was trying to renege, as she knows I will do in a minute; so after the third call in less than thirty minutes I answered her call.

"Hello,"

"Where the fuck are you?" Char bellowed.

"Where the fuck did you call?" I snapped back at her.

"I've been calling you forever, you know the game starts

soon and I still have to pick up Faizon." She growled.

"Char, I need at least another 30minutes." Her response to that comment for sure, sent her blood pressure up.

"Why in dirty hell, do you need an additional half an hour?" She stopped short and took a breath, but continued with her badgering as if she had me on the witness stand. "You know Faizon is slow as hell, so we'll most likely have to wait on her too." I thought I would make a helpful suggestion, by telling her to pick Faizon up first and then pick me up but after it left my mouth, and by Char's charred response, I realized that it was a silly suggestion.

"Why in the hell, would I pick up Faizon first and she lives closest to the arena!?" Even though I had just admitted to her; it was silly, I was getting a little frustrated with Char's attitude so I sarcastically remarked how I didn't have to go at all and could stay home and work throughout the evening.

"Stephon Marbury will understand." I got out before Char yelled through the phone.

"But I won't and you are going! Thirty is all I'm giving you."

"Alright Char, I hear you."

"Lane... be ready!" Char hollered before she hung up.

"I love you Char." All I heard was the dial tone, she was so mad that till this day, I didn't know if she heard me, or if she just hung up on me. I didn't get too bent out of shape, because the fact of the matter is; I did love her and I knew she loved me too. After I thought about how foolish that exchange went, I went back to working on my laptop and focused on my work. I would make the time graciously given to me by Charmine count, because I knew that Char wasn't playing. Finally finished with crunching numbers, I closed my laptop and stared into my closet and thought how those two bitches were going to be catwalk fabulous, and wondered what in the hell was I going to wear? This is a basketball game for crying out loud, I reasoned with myself as I made my selection. I grabbed my fitted Apple Bottom jeans, my black angora off the shoulder tunic and my Jimmy Choo boots. I quickly beveled my fringe and pulled the rest of my hair in a ponytail. I flashed back to Dre and how he used to love to running his hands through my hair; always complimenting me on how my hair always smelled like Pantene. I always wondered how he recognized the smell of Pantene? Did he spy on my side of the cabinets while using the bathroom, or did his sisters use Pantene? By the time I finished putting on my Sheerly Clear lip gloss, Char was at the door yelling for me to hurry up and open the door because she had to pee! When I opened the door just as I thought; the bitch looked like she was auditioning for ANTM about to meet Tyra Banks at the game. I had to admit she was stunning in a Prada silk dress, Fabiani black mink and Chanel boots; but to a game. "Char, don't you think you're a little over dressed for a basketball game?" I asked her.

"Don't worry about me," Char snapped, "just hurry the fuck up!"

"I'm ready," I snapped back. A few moments later, I heard the toilet being flushed and the water running. Char emerged from the bathroom and looked me up and down; snobbishly. "You look good Lane, so you shouldn't hate on me." She smiled and hit me playfully. I replied by telling Char that I wasn't hating on her, I just realized I'm going to a basketball game and not a fashion show. She returned daggered eyes and said, "I know where I'm going, but you just never know who you might meet and I like to be ready for anything." Finally ready to get our night on the road, we jumped into her Platinum Range Rover and headed toward Buckhead to pick up Faizon.

When we arrived at Faizon's, I gave her a quick call to let her know we're outside her gate about to come in, while Charmine punched in the code to enter her gated community. The anxiousness in Faizon's voice made it apparent she wasn't ready. Faizon had left her door ajar for us to come in, but she was nowhere to be found.

"Faizon!" Char hollered.

"I'm in the bathroom!" Faizon returned. I hated to admit it but Char was right, Faizon wasn't near ready. She was in her bathroom struggling to put in her contacts. This infuriated Char to the point I thought she was about to explode. I believe she would have calmed down if Faizon hadn't asked for help in picking out a pair of shoes for her to wear. That did it, I had never actually seen words leave a person's body before, but I did that night. "I AM TIRED OF FUCKING WITH YOU BITCHES, YOU TWO KNEW TWO WEEKS AGO I HAD THESE TICKETS AND THE GAME STARTED AT 7 O'CLOCK! IT'S NOW 8:15, AND YOU STILL DON'T HAVE YOUR SHIT TOGETHER!"

Char dismissed herself and proceeded to walk into Faizon's living room and stared out onto her patio. I walked in Faizon's bathroom where she was standing in her mirror looking annoyed with herself. She whispered to me, "Please find me a pair of black heels while I get this contact in so we can leave. I don't want to have to curse Charmaine's ass out tonight." I walked into her closet and scanned her shoe choices. This chick has shoes galore, but the good thing was she had them all cataloged with a photo in the front of each box so I can see what the hell I was selecting. I picked out what I thought was a nice black pair to go with her outfit. I took one shoe into the bathroom for her approval; she nodded in agreement and asked for another three minutes. That sounded so familiar and I go plop myself onto her couch, as Char is still standing at the patio in deep thought. I gave Char the update on Faizon, told her to relax and assured her that we'll be in her truck in the next 10 minutes.

I knew Char was pissed because she was stone silent; one of her trademarks I hate. I guess because that was the opposite of how I react to stressful situations. When I was angry, the whole world had to suffer. Faizon finally got the contacts in and slipped into the shoes I picked out for her before she walked out of her bedroom, and beckoned us to come on, as if we were her subjects. When we got into the truck, the tension was so thick you could cut it with a knife. I said a silent prayer because I didn't like to ride with them like this. The Lord must have heard my prayer, because after riding through three dead silent lights, one of Char's favorite songs, "Knocking boots" came on the radio. She started singing and even reminisced on how she lost her virginity to Pratt off this very song. "Lane, do you remember Pratt... I wonder why we didn't make it?" Char asked.

"Aahh... maybe because of that little issue of 25 to life." I reminded her.

"Oh yeah… but he was still fine as hell." She remembered, and continued to sing her heart out while Faizon sat quietly in the back looking in her compact mirror. I just sat and stared out the window trying to recall if I had turned off my beveling iron.

After the song went off, Char adjusted her rearview mirror to get a better look at Faizon. She informed the both of us that the only way we could get back in her good graces was if we agreed to buy her beers at the arena, it was a small price to pay for the tension to disappear so I agreed straightaway. It took Faizon, who thinks she is the original Black Barbie a little more convincing, but she eventually agreed. I can't hate though, Faizon's waist is about as small if not smaller than Barbie's. I closed my eyes and quietly thanked God for Him allowing the tension to ease up and making the remainder of our drive quite pleasant. Char found a spot to park and rushed us out, reminding us that we were already late. Once inside the arena, we were ushered to our seats by the arena staff. I couldn't believe how close we were to the floor, now I know why those two were dressed catwalk fabulous. Sky-cams were everywhere, and if it happened to catch them, they would be TV ready.

We got comfortable and I realized the Knicks were winning 24-18, so I was happy. And my man Stephon Marbury was not letting me down. I always had to big up #3 since we're both from Brooklyn. Just at that moment, not only is he stripped of the ball by Speedy Claxon of the Knicks; Claxon scored the point and the arena went wild as if Michael Jordan was in the building. Sky cam swept the arena and there he was; the finest man I knew I would ever see! I mean he was the kind of brother that literally took your breathe away. Frantically, I elbowed Char.

"Did you see that?" I asked her damn near hyperventilating.

"See what?" Char retorted, taking her sweet time looking in the direction of where I pointed.

"Him!", and I continued to wag my freshly manicured finger and point in the direction of the larger than life picture of my future husband. By the time Char got her eyes focused to where I pointed, he was gone! It was precisely at that second, I knew I would make it my life's mission to find him before we left the Phillips. I asked Char had she brought binoculars, "No girl," she snarled. "You know I don't spend my money on shit like that." I was always puzzled why she complained about spending money, when she had everything a girl could want;

don't let the latest Louey V bag or Jimmy Choo shoes come out; she was on the hunt. I didn't begrudge her, she deserves everything she has; she works hard and she enjoys living well. Faizon shouted across Char to tell me that there was a Kiosk that sells binoculars and other souvenirs. She added she just couldn't tell me exactly where the kiosk was located. "Thanks Faizon." I said gratefully as I headed towards the nearest kiosk; so I could just get one more glimpse of him.

I was about to give up on the binoculars when I spotted the stand that was selling a little bit of everything. I grabbed and paid for my second pair of eyes and I'm officially on the prowl. I hauled ass back to my seat to start looking in the direction of where I remembered the Sky cam catching fans enjoying the game. There were so many people here. Discouraged, I wondered how I was going to find him. I did remember he was wearing a black shirt, and adorned to be what looked like a platinum chain with pendant, his hair was either braided or in loc's as it was pulled back off his beautiful chocolate face. Fuck that, if I'm the last one to leave the arena, I'm determined to see him again tonight! Enjoying the game now was virtually out of the question.

Faizon and Char kept trying to include me in their conversation, but I wasn't interested and when Char realized this, she reminded me that this was "Girls night out." I felt bad how I ignored them for a man I would probably never see again and even if I did; who's to say he would want to hook up, hell he could be at the game with his wife and kids for all I know. So I put the binoculars down, and just as I started to enjoy the game Char reminded us of our promise of her free drinks. Faizon firmly stated she wasn't taking another step in her heels until we leave. "Just wait until we get to Dugan's, then I will keep my end of the deal." Faizon informed Char. I had missed so much of the game looking for the man I wanted to father my children, I volunteered to go on the beer run. I told the both of them I would be right back. Faizon asked me to bring her back a beer, I told her to wait until we get to Dugan's. We both had a laugh about that and I headed off to the concession stand. I'm getting closer to the concession stand and wished I'd waited. The lines were crazy long. I almost turned around, but just the thought of hearing Char start her whining prevented me from turning back, so I just got in line and waited patiently.

I was glad to see that even though the lines were long, it was moving fairly quickly. I decided I'd better get my money out now so I wouldn't be the cause of holding up the line. I fumbled around in my bag until I finally get to my wallet, and in my haste, a twenty-dollar bill falls to the floor. As I bent down to pick it up, my hand is met by a dark chocolate hand, attached to a dark chocolate voice. "You dropped this," the voice says. Appreciative that the person didn't take off running with my money, I looked up to say thanks; only to see that it was the Adonis I had been searching for all night, and as fate would have it, here we are. Nervously, I took my money and said "thank you", but something happened to us when we looked in each other's eyes. I promise you, it was almost spiritual. There was an undeniable, passionate connection, which pierced my soul; causing us to be suspended in time. We just stood there staring in each other eyes so long that I didn't even hear when the man called for next in line. Jarred back to earth, I turned to place my order. "Aahh… let me have a two beers and a coke." As the man leaves the counter to prepare my order, I felt the hairs on the back of my neck stand up just knowing that he was standing behind me. I can't believe that I'm speechless after the way I searched for him, even going as far as to buy binoculars. The salesman at the concession stand returned and gave me my total." $12.50", the young man says. I went to hand him my twenty and I heard him from behind me, "I got her and add another two beers." I stammered but manage to get out, "No! Thanks, but no thanks, I got it.", but my future husband insisted.

"No doubt you can pay for it, but please allow me to do this for the finest woman I've seen here tonight. By the way my name is Clay." He extended his hand for me to shake. I literally felt my face warming up. I told him "Thank you" and took his hand, "I better get back to my seat." I announced, and turned to walk away. Are you joking? I so chickened out I thought secretly. I took a few steps and suddenly I felt the gentlest touch on my bare shoulder. I turned around slowly to see if this was a figment of my imagination.

"What's yours?"

"Huh?"

"What's your name?"

"Oooh... Lane."

"Elaine?"

"No Lane, L-A-N-E."

"Oh okay, nice meeting you Lane. Lane, I don't want you to feel obligated because I paid for your refreshments, but would you mind giving me your number?" I must have looked at him like I was a deer caught in some headlights, because he added quickly he would give me his also. He acknowledged that today; a woman wanted to able to reach the man as well, and he let out this laugh that lit his face up. Honestly I wasn't thinking that but hell; if he wanted me to have his number by gosh I was going to take it. I reached back inside my bag and handed him my business card while he went into his wallet and handed me his.

I took a quick glance at the card and turned my attention back to him "Call me on my cell anytime," he said. While he pointed out his office and cell numbers, I was looking at him just thinking about how good he looked and smelled. He was about 6'1, with a chocolate chiseled face, his teeth was so white I thought they were airbrushed, and he adorned the most lustrous loc's I had ever seen on a man. He also had that thug swagger, which has always been a turn on for me and partly the downfall with some of my relationships, but there's nothing like a man with a confident swagger and in a nutshell; I've got to have them. After we exchanged cards, we had that awkward silence. I could have stood there for an eternity, but he finally spoke. "Well, Lane, I'm looking forward to hearing from you real soon." He flashed a smile that made my left knee buckle. I looked back into his eyes and said as seductively as I could, "You sure will hear from me," and I turned and walked off like Loretta Divine did in "Waiting to Exhale", when she knew Gregory Hines was watching her walk off.

I had only taken a few steps when Clay's deep, silky voice called my name. I chuckled to myself as I thought he can't already be hooked; or could he? I turned slowly, walked back, and asked him did he forget something? "No, but you did", and hands me my drinks.

"Thank you." I muttered from embarrassment. With my pride taking a hit, I grabbed my drinks and walked the hell back to my seat. When I reached my seat I'm sitting, but I'm floating at the same time. Angrily Char looked at me not even realizing that I have just seen heaven.

"Where the fuck did you go and what took you so long!? I thought you were brewing the shit yourself, I was about to send Faizon looking for your ass!" Faizon looked away from the game long enough to snap, "The fuck you say, you wasn't sending me no where!" Faizon quickly returned her attention to the game. "Shut up, I was only playing with your ass!" Char responded. While those two had their childish spat, I was dying inside to tell Char what just happened, but Faizon was with us. Now don't get me wrong, I love Faizon, but the chick is negative as sin and I never liked sharing anything with her unless it's was fact. When you tell Faizon you've met someone; her favorite saying is, "Girl, he just wants some pussy!" Char still couldn't let go of the fact I spent so much time getting the drinks, and asked me again what took me so long. "I'll talk to you later Char," I said now disgusted with the both of them.

With my face beaming, I turned to watch what little of the game was left. Thinking about my encounter with Clay, and how embarrassed I was that I almost forgot the drinks, I got nervous that I might've dropped his card as well. In a panic; I snatched my bag open to locate it. I tossed over old tissues, coins, and once I had it in my hands, I took it out to get a closer look. It read, "Clay Roberts Platinum Plus Records." Oh hell no, I blurted out, releasing a disappointed sigh. He looks too old be starting a rap career, Damn! Now don't get me wrong; he was gorgeous but he looked to be in his thirties, the perfect age, because I thought we were about the same age, give or take a few years. I continued to look at the card and read further and spotted CEO. Yes, he's the CEO! Now that is more like it, a man with a sense of ownership; that's always attractive in a man.

I looked at Faizon and Char who were truly enjoying themselves. yet all I could think about was how I couldn't wait for girls night out to be over so I could start a new day, and take Clay up on his call him anytime offer. Could my night get any better? New York beat the hell out of Atlanta 112-93. Happy as a Girl Scout with a new badge, we left the arena and headed for Dugan's. The ride there was quiet; Char and I didn't want to rub the win in Faizon's face because she's a Georgia Peach; a true Southern Belle. At Dugan's we're seated near a table of good looking gentlemen who brought our first round of drinks after they found out we were Knicks fans as well. Faizon kept quiet about the fact she was a Hawks fan, so she could also partake in the spirit of the night. Faizon and I thanked Char for getting the tickets. I had a great time, my team won and I met my husband all in the same night. What more could I ask for?

I couldn't wait until we took Faizon home, so I could tell Char about Clay. We enjoyed one more round and decided to leave. Other than the table of fine men, Dugan's was dead. When we got to Faizon's house, she thanked Char again. "You're welcome. Am I picking up on Sunday for our day at Spa-dells?" Char asks Faizon.

"No, I better drive myself, Darnell may spend the weekend with me so…"

"Yeah you're right, you better drive cause I'm not waiting on you if he plans to come over." Char interrupted.

"Are we doing brunch?" Faizon asked. I quickly aborted that idea because depending on my phone conversation with Clay tomorrow, I could have plans. "Let's play it by ear" I said. Char echoed the same and informed us, it's only because she has tons of work to be finished by Monday. We said our good nights, and blew our imaginary kisses.

Char asked me did I want to stop for something to eat before she took me home, and what the hell have I been dying to tell her all night. I turned down the offer of something to eat and asked her how she knew I was dying to tell her something. "Lane, you know I've known you much too long, not to know when something's on your mind. Your eyes starts dancing in your head like you're doing crack." She laughed. I had to laugh myself; it felt like my eyes were darting between her and Faizon while at Dugan's. "Well Char, you're right I met the love of my life tonight at the game." Char got stone silent, before she finally cautiously spoke.

"Lane, I don't want you to get your hopes up, you remember what happened to the last love of your life."

"Stop bringing up old shit!" I snapped. Clay is an amazing man and he's different."

"You would know that how? You just met him and his name is Clay, what kind of name is that?"

"He owns his own company."

"What, a play dough company?" Char cracked her own self up with laughter.

"No, he's the CEO of a record label."

"And you discovered all of this out when?"

"When I went on the beer run, I first saw him on the sky cam. Do you remember when I was nudging you to look?"

"Oh yeah; the urgency for the binoculars."

"Right, but there were so many people, plus I couldn't remember exactly where I saw him, so I gave up. And then lo and behold I go to get our drinks and there he is!" I pulled his card out from my bag.

"Look Char, here's his card." Char takes the card out of my hand to inspect it closer; peering very suspiciously, she gives it back and shook her head in disapproval.

"What's the problem?" I asked.

"Nothing's wrong Lane."

"No Char, just say it." She hesitated and sighed heavily before she started.

"Alright Lane, I don't want to seem as if I'm not happy for you but anybody can get cards made up, hell; we used to and we were barely out of college."

"I know that Char, do you think I'm a fucking sped!" Getting somewhat annoyed. "He told me to call him anytime, cell or office. Do you think he would tell me that if he was passing out fake cards!?"

"Look, I'm sorry. I don't mean to sound uncaring but we both have traveled this road before." Char whispered. "I thought the breakup with Dre was going to kill you. I can't... won't just sit back and watch you at that level of despair again." I listened to every word that Char is pouring out to me, because I never thought I could experience that kind of pain from a man. "No Char, it should be me apologizing, you're right; I know you only have my best interest at heart. I promise to take this slow, it may not even lead to anything but a phone call, but it's just that something magical happened tonight and I just want to see where it will take me if anywhere."

"Thanks for understanding Lane, I just love you, you're more than a friend, you're my sister without the bloodline."

"Girl you know I feel the same way; that's why I know I'll be careful because I don't want you to have to sit with me days on end like you did with the Dre saga. The rest of the way home we talked about how the Knicks kicked the shit out of the dying Hawks. Charmine dropped me off in front of my house and reminded me that she has a shit load of work to do, so her phone would be off most of the day but I could always call her on her emergency number if I needed her, and she stresses the word emergency. I thanked her for her part in the night and skipped into my house like a teenager coming from prom.

Relay-tionships

Chapter Three

I woke up a little after 10 the next morning, and started getting ready for the day like I had a hot date. I showered quickly and slipped on something silky. I lay across my Mahogany four-poster bed and pulled Clay's card out of my bag. At first I just stared at it, not really sure what I was going to do as I recapped our conversation from last night. I almost had an orgasm when I remembered how gentle his touch was on my shoulder. I looked at his card and decided it was now or never. I called his office number first just to hear his voice, it was Saturday so I did not expect him to be there. Just as I thought…answering machine comes on. "Hello, you have reached Clay Roberts at Platinum Plus records; please leave your name and number, and I or one of my associates will get back with you. Bless." I hung up without leaving a message. Butterflies have now found a new home in my stomach. Damn! He sounds even better over the phone. I closed my eyes just to picture him again standing there in that black shirt, against his dark skin. Yes, I'm going to pursue this, I only live once I convinced myself.

I wrote a few lines in my journal before I decided to call his cell. I closed my journal and headed for my living room to put on some Marvin Gaye and pour me a glass of red wine before I make that call. I continued to sip my wine, and walked back towards my bedroom to retrieve his number I left on my bed when my phone rings. It startled me so I picked up without even checking my caller ID. Answering in my, it's just anybody voice "Hello."

"Hello, this is Clay returning a call." How the fuck… I'm totally scattered now.

"Oh Clay, this is Lane it was me who called but your machine was on, and I, …

"Oh Lane good morning. I had my office calls routed to my cell." His voice appeared to get smoother when he realized it was me.

"Ok, I was wondering how you knew, I didn't bother to leave a message."

"Why you didn't just call my cell, I told you I wanted to hear from you." Did he just say" want" and "you" in the same sentence? Slow down Lane I told myself, allow him to make his intentions known.

"I know you must be a busy man; with you being the chief in your own company." I just wanted to call, but decided I could wait."

"Lane as good as you look… you shouldn't have to wait on anything, or anyone. I'm glad you decided to call, but you're right about one thing. I am a busy man; my associate and I are about to meet a potential client, so if I could call you later."

"Oh Clay, no more needs to be said, of course you can call me later."

"What is a good time for you?" I had to stop myself from

saying- I was like the waffle house open 24 hours, but instead I said quite reserved, "Well... I'm having dinner with some college friends who are in town for the weekend, so anytime after nine is good, if that's not to late for you?"

"Yeah actually that sounds great, I'm sure I'll be done by that time and I can devote my undivided to you."

"Well it's a wrap, I'll hear from you soon Clay."

"Tonight, bless." I repeated `bless` back to him and hung up the phone.

What the hell would make me tell him that I was having dinner with friends? I asked myself heading back to the living room as I gulped the remainder of my wine, only to pour myself another glass. I'm elated as hell and I only talked to him over the phone, imagine if he was next to me? Wait... I wondered was he happy to hear from me; or did he think I was a potential client and felt obligated to call back, but why did he say he was happy to hear from me. Stop it; don't start this insane, insecure bullshit I mentored to myself. You must know an Adonis like Clay; women are plenteous, so easy does it and relax! I was hoping that my self-help techniques would kick in and start working, but why did I have to say call after nine, that was the entire day I had to wait for his call.

I decided to give Char a call to see what she's doing, and hoped she would want to hangout to help me kill some time until Clay called back. I dialed her number, and she picked up after a couple of rings.

"What's up Char?"

"What's up girl?"

"What are you doing?"

"Nothing Lane. What's up with you?" I could hear Char's voice is growing impatient, so I stopped hedging with my small talk.

"Guess what?"

"You called the sandman and what happened?" She jokes.

"Ha-ha Char, his name is Clay." I heard Char's continued snickering. "

"Stop being so sensitive; I'm just fucking with you."

"I know."

"Well, how did it go?"

"Good." We didn't get to talk long. He was scheduled to meet with a hopeful client within a few hours. He told me he was happy to hear from me, and he'd call me back after my dinner date with my old college friends."

"Oh, and who would that be Lane?"

"I lied, but I was hoping..."

"Nope," Char shouted before I could get the rest out of my mouth." I got tons of shit to do, like I told you last night; as it is I'm going to miss half a day of catching up with our spa date and all on tomorrow, and I have a presentation first thing Monday morning. What would make you lie about that?"

"Alright calm down, I just thought you may have wanted to take a break to have some lunch; my treat."

"Don't use me Lane."

"Now why would you say that, you know I'm not using you; I know you're hungry."

"Listen heifer, I can treat my own self to lunch and most of all I don't want to hear you talk endlessly about a man you barely know."

"Alright, you're right... you caught me. I did want to kill some time."

"I know I'm right, so I'll talk to your ass in the morning.

You driving or am I picking you up?"

"No I'll drive, I'm going to head out for a jog after the spa."

"Cool, see you at the Spa."

"10, right?"

"Right, and Lane; I'm about to turn my phone off so don't forget, call me only if there's an emergency." She stressed her point.

"I won't. See you tomorrow." Disconnected, I'm frustrated that it didn't go as planned. What am I going to do with all this time to myself? I looked at my watch and it is only 12:35. The combination of wine and Marvin got me buzzed in a nice way. I opened my blinds, threw myself across my leather sofa, and daydreamed about the next time I would see Clay. Where would we go? What would I wear? Allowing myself to drift with Marvin, I imagined Clay caressing my face, seducing me with his beautiful, long lashed chestnut eyes, kissing my neck and shoulders until his tongue invades my mouth. It was almost as if I could smell him in my thoughts. As he undressed me slowly, he tells me how badly he wants me. I felt my body shake from a warm sensation that snapped me right back in my living room on my sofa.

I might as well get some jogging in today; I was much too excited to sit at home the rest of the day waiting for his call. I just can't seem to shake my insecurities about my size, even with all the compliments from good looking men and women. If I could only lose about 5 to 10 more pounds. I know this is my personal hang up, but Clay sure didn't seem to mind my size, he approached me first; he must have been attracted. I changed into my jogging attire and headed out to the park for my jog. It was such a clear day, I might as well kill some time there. I threw on my Nikes before I grabbed my keys and headed out the door. Taking the scenic route to Piedmont Park,

I appreciate what a perfect day it was for jogging; not too cold, and the scenery is awesome for mind clearing. I reached my destination and started looking for a spot where I could do my warm ups before I started my jog. Pass some kids playing Frisbee with their dog, I found the perfect spot and got busy.

Putting my iPod in, I noticed I had an admirer to the left of me, he looked just alright, and I really just wanted to jog. I finished my last set of warm ups before I started a slow jog around the park. I noticed my admirer has not only started to jog; but has slowed down his pace. By the time I reached him, he jogged at my pace to keep in time with me. We gave each other the cordial jog smile and nod, I proceeded to focus on my music and jog. Our second time around the park, my admirer got the courage to motion to me to take my earplugs out; I obliged but continued to jog at my same pace. "Hi" he says, I say hi back and give him a quizzical look as if to say "What the hell." He doesn't catch on as, he proceeded to hold a conversation.

"Good day for jogging."

"Yeah it is a nice day." I responded in a friendly, but not too friendly tone.

"I'm Trevor."- I know he isn't slowing me down- just to tell me his name.

"Nice meeting you Trevor, I don't want to appear rude, but I'm just here for a jog; plus I'm in a committed relationship." Did I just say committed relationship and who was I talking about...Clay? What Trevor says next abruptly brings me back to reality.

"Hey, I was just being friendly; I didn't ask you to marry me."

"I know you didn't, and I was just trying not to be rude,

because I really wanted to tell you to fuck off!" I snarled sarcastically before I gave my park admirer a smile, and peeled off leaving him to get a good look at my ass. Did I just tell that idiot I was in a committed relationship? Am I bugging or what? Just let me run the track once more, and I'm out. I will find something at home to dwindle the time away. After my run, I went to have a smoothie before heading home.

As I am driving through the city, I admired how beautiful the scenery was. The leaves are crisp, with the brightest colors of orange and hues of red. Once inside my house, I'm feeling gritty and sweaty, I knew I needed to shower again from my run. I gathered a load of clothes before going through my mail; I've been too busy to read during the week. shower. Once my last few tasks is done, I'm shower bound. I'm in the shower and completely lathered when I heard the phone ring. I debated if I should answer it. I knew it wasn't anywhere nearing 9 o'clock yet, so it can't be Clay. It crossed my mind that it could be Char wanting to apologize for her rude behavior earlier, so I decided to let it go to voice mail. I started washing my hair when the phone started ringing again. Shit, it may be important or it had better be, I thought to myself; pissed off with shampoo finding my eyes.

"Hel-lo." I answered, intentionally sounding as annoyed as I can be.

"Hello Lane?"

"Clay, I didn't expect you to call so early."

"Did I catch you at a bad time?"

"Aahh honestly, yes you did. I'm standing here dripping wet, I was in the shower."

"Oh really, can I join you?" He asks.

"Yes." What did I just say, Clay is silent on the other end, did he hear me and what will he think of me now? "Clay, are you still there?"

"Yeah I'm here; I thought I heard you say yes; I could join you." Now what you gonna say? You put yourself on Front Street now let me see how you'll get off. I wondered to myself.

"Yes, you did hear me right, but I think that was two glasses of wine I had earlier speaking for me."

"Lane, you don't have to blame it on the wine. Check it, I know you're standing there wet so to get to the point; I was calling to invite myself to dinner with you and your friends tonight, my client was a no show and I'm free"

"Dinner?"

"Yeah, with you and your friends."

"Friends?"

"Yeah, you said you were having dinner with some of your friends from school." Clay's call had thrown me way off. In a second, I forgot what the fuck I told him earlier, and he caught on to the bullshit. While I stood there stark naked and dripping wet, and not knowing what to say...he did. "Lane, you said it best earlier, I'm a very busy man, too busy to play games. If you didn't want to be bothered just simply say it, I'm good with that." I laid my towel on my bed to have a seat and find a way to redeem myself.

"Clay, allow me to apologize to you and start over with the truth this time. Yes, I would love to have dinner with you tonight minus my friends, because I was never having dinner with old friends. I just didn't want you to think I didn't have a life, so I lied about my evening; please forgive me?" He didn't respond for a minute, and I resolved to whatever he said when he decided to speak, I deserved it. "Lane, of course I'll forgive you, and I'm glad we won't be dining with your friends because that makes just the two of us." My heart dropped, I will be having dinner with him. My thoughts started to race on, what am I going to wear, my hair. Clay told me to finish my shower, then text him with my address, and a good time for him to pick me up. I assured him I would do just that, as soon as we got off the phone. I hopped my ass back in the shower with a brand new outlook on life. I'm so excited; I damn near loofahed my ass raw.

Contemplating if I had time to buy an outfit, I realized I didn't. No time for that; let me just find something I already have in my closet. As I conditioned my hair, I mentally scanned my closet, pants or dress. I'll wear a dress, which dress? He saw me in black last night, yeah but that was just a black shirt. Eager, I jumped out of the shower so I could really get the night started. I tore through my closet most of which is black, my signature color. I made what I thought was a ravishing first date outfit. And since I didn't know where he was taking me, it was appropriate for any place. I pulled out my DKNY wrap dress, with my DKNY boots. Killer, I thought as I started to work on my hair. I looked at the time; it was only minutes after 4 pm so I could be ready by 7 because my hair had to be right. That was nearly three hours away and gave me more than enough time to add my finishing touches. I had to call Char; not to rub it in her face but to let her know that Clay is not only interested, but he initiated our dinner date for the evening.

I threw on my robe and wrapped my hair to finish drying. I dialed her number and each time it went to voice mail. Where is she and why isn't she answering her phone? I didn't want to call her on her emergency line, but she really was leaving me no choice. Completely forgetting about her only request for the night, I dialed her emergency number and she picked up without hesitation. Once I heard her voice, I knew I made the wrong decision in calling her emergency line, she picked up the line nervously.

"Lane are you..."

"Yeah Char I'm fine."

"No bitch wrong answer, something needs to be wrong with you if you called me on this line."

"I just wanted to let you know that Cla...." Char was furious; she didn't permit me to go further. "Clay, are you bullshitting me? Lane, I told you I have mountains of work I need to have completed for Monday, and you called on my dire emergency line about some fucking dude you half met last night. Look I better hang up before I say some real foul shit to you, I'm hanging up!" And that's exactly what she did. I didn't have a chance to say anything. I sat on my bed dumbfounded with the phone in my hand for a few minutes before I text's Clay with the information he needed to pick me up. With my outfit picked out I just had to concentrate on my hair, the decision was simple; I wore it down with that dress. I looked in my four way mirror at the end result, if I lost like 5 pounds, I could be a pin-up; but damn...I still look good. I changed my mind about my boots and stepped into some black heels. Pleased with my shoe choice, I admired my legs a little longer. Yeah that's more like it my legs look better in these shoes, and he can see the shape of my legs better. Not a hair out of place, I put on my favorite fragrance by Christian Dior and thought how someone could look this good; be poison. I smiled to myself at the thoughts I had and headed up front to pour a glass of red and waited for my date. The phone rang and it's Clay.

"Clay."

"Hello Lane, I'm about 20 minutes away, do you want

anything before I reach you?"

"No, I don't need anything.

"Lane, I didn't ask you if you needed anything, I asked you if you wanted something; there's a difference." I grinned and rephrased it for him.

"No thanks Clay, I don't want anything but you, see you in twenty." He chuckled, told me less than and hung up. I gulped my wine and ran to the bathroom to put on my Fashion Fair lip-gloss and gave myself a heart to heart in the mirror. "Look Lane this is your first date, and he is not like the rest; so leave Dre, Greg, and Antoine at home. I licked my lips and checked my hair one last time before grabbing my bag out of my bedroom. He'll be here any minute so I walked into the living room putting things in their proper places. I put my wine back in my cabinet and cleared the few scattered dishes that was on the table in the living room. I forgot my cell phone in my bedroom and ran back to get it, no sooner than I got back up front and put my phone in my bag, my doorbell rings. I took a deep breathe, smoothed out my dress and opened the door for my guest.

When I opened the door and saw him, the earth stood still for sure, the finest man I know I have ever seen is standing there.

"Hi Lane... you're gorgeous." He greeted me and walked in. He took one hand to grab me around my waist and kissed me on the cheek. I closed my eyes and took in his scent, before I returned his greeting. "Hello Clay, you look good yourself." And that he did, from head to toe in a crisp white shirt, some jeans, Crockett & Jones shoes and platinum chain. His loc's were still pulled back off his chocolate face, and a sexy ass goatee. Some women liked the smooth as a baby's ass face on a man, not me; hair on a man was mad sexy.

"Clay, may I offer you something to drink?"

"No, I'll wait until we get to Houston's, is Houston's alright with you, if not you can choose someplace different?"

"No, Houston's is fine; they make a wonderful corn soup I love."

"Well if you're ready..."

"I'm ready. I grabbed my coat from the closet. Clay took it from me and assisted me in putting it on. I turned off my lights and locked the door behind us.

I am officially on a date I mused. I walked out of my house to see the newest model Benz parked in my driveway, just what I expected; this man has done very well for himself. And guess what, I'm with him! He opened my door and waited for me to be seated before he closed my door. Clay entered his car and when he got in; he looked at me, but said nothing. As I'm looked back at him, I wondered what it would be like to fuck this man. It was as if he heard what I was thinking, because at that moment he reached over to me, still not saying a word; he placed his hand behind my neck, pulled me gently towards him and started to kiss me. I accepted him in my mouth like we had been dating for some time. His tongue felt so warm and tasted so good. He took his other hand and found my waist through my unbuttoned coat and pulled my body as close to him as we could get while still in his car. I placed my hand on his neck and caressed it while I kissed him with all the passion I felt radiate from my body. I felt his hands wanting to explore, but wanting to be respectful at the same time. I felt my pussy throb with the desire of wanting him inside me. God, he felt so good! I could feel his manhood come alive, and he knew it too and that's when he pulled me into him for the last time, before ending the gentlest kiss I've had in a very long time. He took his hand from around my waist and placed it on the steering wheel. Refusing to take his eye off me, he finally confessed he had wanted to kiss me from last night. He started the car and we're on our way to Houston's. Clay asked me if I want the heat on. Was he not there? I was already heated; my body was still in flames by his touch. "No Clay, I'm fine." He took his eyes off the road, looked at me and said, "Yes you are." I smiled and sat back, feeling ever so comfortable with him. We talked a little about our background on the drive there.

He asked me about my move from the Big Apple to the Peach State. I lied and said it was a career move, I could never tell him that I was sent packing by a love that went awry. He told me all about his childhood dream of wanting to have his own record label, and all of the blood, sweat and tears it took to get it, but the bottom line was he did it. I learned that he was the only male raised in a household of three strong women, his mother, grandmother, and sister. He said he met his father only twice, he admitted regretfully; both times ended in disaster. He added that he realized at that point he could only control his behavior, and chose not to try to fix a relationship, that was so poorly severed.

He talked about the respect he has for his mother, big ma, and his "Sissy" Keisha, he calls them his Treasured Trio.

"Lane, I don't want to sound like I'm tooting my own horn but there are some things I want you to know about me. I'm a man, I work hard for everything I have, and everything I'll ever have. I know how to treat a woman; my big ma and moms made sure of that. That's why when I asked you earlier did you "want" something and you said "need," it threw me because I'm a man, so you'll always have what you need. I want to give you your wants, and if I can do that; I'm successful. My God, I'm in love. No man has EVER said that to me! He looked me straight in my eyes while he talked to me and I felt he was being sincere. I wondered how, why is this man not with someone, but who said he doesn't have someone. Even though I would find that hard to believe if he didn't; I had to find that out before I allowed myself to get too deep. This is a man I could easily love with everything I have, but this time I've got to be one hundred percent sure. We arrived at Houston's and valet parked. He escorted me out of the car and into the restaurant. Clay asked me if I would like a drink at the bar before dinner. "Yes, I would like a glass of red." Not wanting to mix my drink of the evening, and Clay orders a shot of Hennessey, which I discovered later on, is his signature drink.

While waiting on our drinks; Clay asked me about my family. I told him I'm the only child of two wonderful parents that are still living in New York; I shared with him the very close relationship we all share. I talked a little about how my father was not very educated, but how he walked over hot coals to provide nothing but the best for my mother and I. I spoke of how he made sure my education was priority, and it's because of his encouragement; I graduated top of my class and now I'm reaping the benefits of a great career, and great home. I did not want to get too deep on the first date but I told him that my mother had cancer but she was in remission. He listened so intently as I talked, he made me feel like nothing else mattered. When I finished he told me he was sorry to hear that my mother had cancer but was happy to hear she was in remission. He commented on the statement I made about my dad not being very educated, but made the point that my dad was smart enough to make sure I had all the tools to live well. I said I'd never looked at it like that before and from that day till now, I have never used the words uneducated, or father in the same breath. Our drinks came and we talked about the ATL vs. NY game. Clay told me he was going to convert me to becoming a Hawks fan. Laughing; I told him, "Never!" He informed me that he almost didn't make the game. He asked me had I gone to the game by myself; I was more than happy to tell him that my best friend got us the tickets from one of her business partners who was called out of the country unexpectedly, and knew Char appreciated basketball. He leaned in, touched my knee, and said how glad he was that he did make it, and Char got the tickets. I rubbed his goatee, a pretense as if he had something in it, when really all I wanted was to touch his face. Before I took my hand from his face; he grabbed my hand and kissed it. Alright, this is the perfect time to ask the "Why" question.

"Clay, may I ask you something?"

"Sure, what do you want to know."

"I don't want to assume anything so I won't... are you in a relationship?"

"Not at the moment. I was but I ended it." Whew, I thought, the chick that let him go was a dumb ass; but thank God for her fuck up.

"Do you want to talk about it?" I pried.

"No, I'm with you tonight and that's what it is." I was trying to read his face, was he still in love, was he bitter, was he rebounding? Nothing, I couldn't read anything. After our drinks, we were escorted to our table by a young lady which I could smell the envy coming from her pores. She seated us, but had ignored me from the moment she said, "Follow me please." She asked Clay did we have any drink orders coming from the bar? He told her no, so she handed Clay the menus and asked him was he ready to order, or did he need more time. And each time Clay looked at me and asked me if I was ready to order, or did I need to look at the menu. I knew exactly what I wanted but out of spite, I had Clay send her on her way until

I looked over the menu. I toyed with the menu for a few minutes and told Clay I'm ready to order.

Clay got our server's attention to come back over to take our order. She's now added a little extra in the swaying of her hips as she walked over, and continued to treat me like I was invisible. Clay decided he would have the baked Salmon with roasted potatoes and vegetables. I decided to have Salmon as well, but kept true to the game and had my corn soup. I watched him as he ordered our food trying to see if I could find something that reminded me of Dre. Dre was also a good looking specimen, but he had nothing on Clay. The only similarities so far were their hands; they both had nice strong looking hands. I got a taste of how strong Clay hands were, while he was holding me so tightly in his car. I now wondered was he kissing me, or her. In all honesty, it truly didn't matter like he said; he was with me tonight. Am I sick or what, I'm sitting across from a man so fine, our waitress looks as if she'd poison my soup just to sit with him. He has his own company, respectful of women, it's evident he has his shit together and all I can think about is, are there any similarities to a man I caught in the act of eating another bitches pussy in our bed, all the while; professing his love for me. Who is sicker me or Dre? Well, there went my pep talk out the window, get a grip Lane. I reminded myself of the chit-chat I had with myself before leaving my house. Clay asked me if I was all right, he noticed I was being quiet. "Clay, I'm good. I'm just enjoying the evening and admiring you." He gave me this half smile that was so sexy and said he was thinking the same thing. While waiting on our dinner to be brought to our table, Clay admitted to me that he was turned off by my lie about having dinner with friends, and asked if I made it a habit to lie. I assured him that, that was not my style and I regretted telling him that unnecessary tale. Finally the server returns to our table with our food, she served us and asked Clay would he be needing anything else?

"Do you want anything else Lane?"

"No Clay, this will do for now." I looked the server dead in her eyes and smirked. The evening was perfect; Clay and I talked, laughed, and continued to have a much enthralled conversation about any and everything that popped in our heads. I had forgotten how much fun I could have and be so at ease with a person I barely knew. Before we knew it, we were the last of two other couples determined to close Houston's. I knew I had my spa date with Faizon and Char in the morning, so even through I hated it, I knew I had to bring this night to a close. When I told Clay of my planned day with the ladies, he asked me were they my imaginary friends, or did I really have a day at the spa planned. "I deserved that Clay, but I really do have plans." I explained how we do this once a month, he laughed and beckoned for our server to bring him the check. "Lane, I want to thank you for making this night so pleasurable. I didn't get the client as I hoped, but I feel I got someone just as important." The check came and he took out his black card, and handed it to the server.

"Clay, I too had a wonderful evening you're a very interesting, attractive man and if I don't hear from you after tonight, just know that you have made me feel very special."

"I'm glad to hear that I made you feel special, but I didn't do anything spectacular it was just dinner, wait until I'm able to plan our next date" He doesn't even realize it, but my prayers have just been answered. He just let me know that there will be a next time. The server returned with his card.

"Thank you Mr Roberts, I hope everything was to your satisfaction." Our server flirted for the last time.

"Yeah it was good, how about you Lane; did you enjoy it."
I looked at him, hoping that he could read between the lines,
and understood me when I said; I loved it!

Clay took my hand and ushered me from my seat, he placed
his hand on the small of my back and lead me out the door.
Since we almost closed the restaurant, the valet driver had
Clay's car in front waiting on us. Clay helped me in the car and
we headed for my house. We didn't have much to say on the
drive back to my house, it was like neither of us really wanted
the night to end, but didn't know how to say it. Finally I spoke
and asked Clay would I know any of his clients? He asked me
was I into hip-hop? When I said yeah, he gave me a funny look.

"Why are you looking at me like that?"

"I didn't think you listened to rap."

"Why?"

"You look more like the neo-soul, jazz type." He informed me.

"Oh really, what does the neo-soul, jazz type woman look
like?" He started laughing, and looked embarrassed by his
comments. "Yeah right, I was judging a book by its cover, and
that's something I hate when it's done to me." I told Clay that
I was a hip-hop fanatic; I even asked him if he could hook me
up with Busta? He found that extremely funny, but did humor
me by saying; he'd see what he could do. Damn, here's my exit
and we would be at my house in a few, I did an insta-sulk.

"Lane, I enjoyed being with you tonight. I'm so happy we
were thirsty at the same time last night; I would not have had
the opportunity of meeting you. You're an intelligent, sexy,
beautiful woman and I would love to see you again if you're
good with that."

"Clay, I would love it, you have my numbers just call me,
and we'll go from there." I really wanted to call Char and

Faizon to cancel my date with them, and just tell Clay he could see me in the morning, because he didn't have to leave. We pulled into my driveway and my sensor lights came on. Clay parked, got out, and rushed to my side to let me out. He walked me to my door and waited for me to open it. When I got the door opened; I turned to say my thank you, and good night to him at the front door. His intention was to come inside and believe me, I didn't have a problem with that. Once we entered my house, he took my coat off and laid it on the back of my sofa. He surprised me by placing his strong hands around my waist as he started to kiss my cleavage and worked his way to my neck. One of his hands has now found my ass and has pulled me so close to him; I could feel his dick making its presence known, for the second time of the night. I took my hand and placed it over his manhood, and slid it slowly against his length to see how much I could excite him. With his growing excitement, I went back to my earlier thoughts of how nice it would be to have him inside me.

The softness of his lips sent electric flutters through my body, he continued to kiss me with such a sensuous fire; I heard myself moan and now allowed him to take full charge of my body. I threw my head back to offer Clay my breasts, which he accepted willingly. He took playful bites at my nipples that have now come through the fabric of my dress. Dazed with passion; I wondered what was I doing, I just met this man, but it is too late, I want to fuck him and now. Feeling my body shiver from his touch, and his mouth still on mine, my pussy is now so wet, I've concluded, I'm ready to receive my lover. Clay looked at me and asked with his eyes is this okay. I gave him his answer by unbuttoning his shirt and I started to kiss his bare chest. I could taste how good he was, and I wanted to make his body quiver with titillation. When

I got to the last button of his shirt, I allowed my tongue to circle his navel, I took pride in hearing him pant in delight as intended. He closed his eyes and rested his head on his neck as I continued to lick his stomach and chest until he stood me directly in front of him. Clay loosened my wrap dress until it exposed my body in full. He stepped back to take me all in; I allowed my dress to slide off my shoulders and down my arms until it hit the carpet. There I stood in my black lace corset, black thigh high stockings, and heels. Clay, who was now leaned on the wine cabinet just admiring what he saw, took my hands and pulled me into him, he slipped his hand in my bra to expose my left breast, and he teased it before he took it in his mouth. God, his mouth felt so warm. I felt my body awaken and I continued to moan from the sheer joy this man was bringing me. I closed my eyes and allowed him to pleasure me until I was so wet that he easily slipped his fingers inside me. He felt my body spasm, and at that moment, a shirtless Clay walked me to the back of my house in search of my bedroom. When he found it, he lifted me gently and laid me onto my bed, I laid still in anticipation for what would happen next. Clay stepped out of his pants to uncover the rest of his chiseled body, giving me time to look at and appreciate his manhood; which was soon about to be freed from his Calvin Klein's. He approached me as I laid on my four poster bed, watching his every move. Tenderly, Clay devoured my nipples while he unhooked my bra, when was off completely, he held it to his nose, inhaled my scent, and placed it with his pants. Lying beside me, Clay took his hands and caressed my pussy until I couldn't take it anymore.

"Lane, are you sure you want to do this?"

"Yes Clay, I just have one request and that is we that we protect ourselves. I have some condoms in my nightstand draw." Clay reached in my nightstand and asked me to put it on. Alluringly, I took off his CK's. Damn! I'm aroused instantly, as I looked at the size of his manhood; his dick was even pretty. It felt so smooth as I guided the condom over what was about to bring me pure intoxication.

"Lane, you had one request and so do I."

"Sure Clay, what is it?"

"That you keep on your stockings and heels while I make love to you." Shit, I love it… he's a freak !

"Yes, I will." Clay rolled my lace panties off my ass as he handled his manhood and found his way to my warmness that awaited him. Clay placed my silky leg on his back and entered me with such desirous thrusts; it caused me to let out a wispy moan. My eyes closed, I felt his warm, and rapid breathes on my neck and his dick taking me to ecstasy. With each thrust, I met him so our bodies were in rhythm. I felt as if I was on the lightest cloud. Clay slid his hand down my leg and grabbed my ass. With what seemed like a blissful eternity; he pulled me into him for the last time before he exploded inside me. In one last motion, he flipped me onto him and I lay still on his chest until I felt him slip out of me. We laid there silently before Clay kissed my forehead and excused himself to my bathroom. No sooner than he's out of sight, I covered my face with shame; what had I done? I just slept with a stranger. Not only was he going think I was a liar, but a ho as well. What the fuck did…

"Lane." Clay called out as I was still reeling from what just happened.

"Yeah Clay, you need… I mean want something" I corrected myself.

"Yeah, I want you to come here." When I stepped into my bathroom, Clay was standing in my walk-in shower holding out his hands, for me to join him. I obliged without any hesitation as we allowed the steaming water to envelop us. Clay took my face in his hands and kissed me sweetly on my lips.

"Lane, I want you to know I didn't intend for what just happened between us to happen, but I don't regret it either. We're adults, and I don't make excuses. What's done is done."

"I'm glad to hear you say that; because it has never been my practice to sleep with a man on the first date, but honestly; I don't have any regrets either. Clay took my body sponge and lovingly washed my body until it was his turn and I returned the favor. When we're finished Clay turned the water off, stepped out of the shower first, grabbed a towel and dried me off, then tucked the towel around his waist. We walked into my room, I glanced over at the time, it was nearly to 3 a.m., and I thought about our spa date in the morning.

After what just took place I should have felt comfortable enough to ask Clay to spend the night, but I didn't want to be too forward, so I let him call the shots. "Lane, it's late and I know you have a busy day later on so I'm going to head out, call me when you get in." I put on my robe, sat on my bed, and watch him get dressed. When he is finished, he walked over to me, pulled me off the bed, and kissed me once more time before having me walk him to the door. "Clay, I had the most fun time with you tonight and I will call you later on, thanks for everything. I opened the door and watched him got into his car and drive off before I closed my door. That was my first encounter with the incredible Mr Clay Roberts, and I prayed that it wasn't my last. I looked so forward to where this night would take us.

Relay-tionships

Chapter Four

I knew I would need to set my alarm to make sure I get up on time. With an evening like I just had, I knew I could easily sleep in. I get into bed and rewound the entire night in my head and thought; what a good time I had. I thought about Clay, and how he is definitely the total package. He seemed so caring, attentive, strong, and respectful. And the way he made love to me, just thinking about it made my body shudder and release deep breaths. Now I just hoped that sleeping with him on the first night didn't scare him off. He said it wouldn't, but I'll see. He asked me to call him tomorrow, but I'll wait to see if he calls me first. Good night, Mr Clay, and I drift into a peaceful sleep. Char calls first thing; before my alarm even went off. "Good morning." Char bellows

"Damn Skippy it is" I respond cheerfully.

"What's up with you, head?"

"Oh nothing… I was about to call to tell you that I couldn't make it today." I await her response playfully; as I know she is about to go off.

"What, Why?"

"Relax, I'm just joking about not coming, but I'm not joking when I tell you I had the best night I've had in almost a year."

"What, from a phone call?"

"See... wrong. I had a date, and that's why I called your ass on your emergency line, but you didn't give me a chance to tell you that my plans had been updated."

"So ole boy came through?"

"Not only did ole boy come through; we went to Houston's where we had a delightful time. We talked and laughed so much; we damn near closed the restaurant, and then we came back here." I could hear Char wanting to ask me for more but was waiting for me to offer the information in her silence.

"Well, I'm glad you had a nice time. You said he came back for drinks?" Char asks.

"No, we didn't drink here; we had drinks at Houston's." I knew what she was getting at; I was just going to play the game with her a little longer.

"Hmmm, alright...what time did he leave?" Bingo! magic question.

"What time did he leave?" I repeat, as if I did not hear her the first time.

"You heard what I asked you!" Laughing, I told Char I was just kidding I heard the question.

"He left about 3 a.m."

"3 o'clock, what the fuck was y'all doing until three, and you better not say fucking!"

"Okay ...I won't say fucking."

"Did you? Char shouts!

"Didn't you just say don't tell you."

"Lane, stop playing these kiddy ass games; did you fuck that man on the first night or not!?"

"Yes Char, we did make love and it was the best night I've had in a long time. It was magical, his shit is huge and he knows how to use it, not like that bitch ass Dre....that big dick minute man."

"Wait; here we go... how did Dre get into this conversation. Lane, it's over between you and Dre, or at least I hoped so. You have got to stop comparing him to other men; I hope you can do that before you dive into a new relationship."

"Of course I can, it's just Dre hurt me so...

"My point exactly, Dre hurt you so badly. I don't even know how he came up, and for real...I don't want to talk about him anymore. Tell me about this Clay."

"Well, of course it is too early to tell, but... I could easily fall in love with him. He seems so sweet, but with that thug swagger that sends me wild, he owns a successful record label, he takes care of his family."

"Family?"

"Yeah, his mother, sister and grandmother."

"Does he have a girlfriend or did you even bother to ask?"

"Of course I asked. He said he was in a relationship, but he was the one who broke it off. He didn't say why; he just said he didn't want to talk about it on our first date."

"Yeah, that makes sense, do you plan to see him again?"

"Shit I hope so, he told me to call him today after our spa date."

"So I guess that rules out brunch."

"Char, you're the one who ruled out brunch on Friday after

the game; claiming you had so much work to do before tomorrow."

"For your information, I finished my presentation yesterday. I only had one person not to honor my don't call request, Lame."

"Shut up Char, and I told you about calling me that."

"You shut up... get your ass up and dressed. I don't want to be late. I'm looking forward to this massage, I truly need it."

"If you had a man; you wouldn't need to look so forward to these monthly massages." I said jokingly.

"Lookey -Lookey at whose got a piece of dick for the first time in over four months, and has now turned into Dear Abby." Char snorts forcefully.

"Char I didn't mean to hurt your feelings."

"You didn't hurt my feelings bitch, I keep telling you and Faizon; I don't need a man to define me apparently as much as y'all two do." I left it alone because I knew what I said was hurtful, especially knowing how long it took Char to be able to get to the place she's at now, after her relationship with Kamel ended. She added she was going to call and wake Faizon's sleepy ass too, and she would meet us in Buckhead. I'm up, energized to start getting ready for our day. Clay had wet my hair while we showered last night, so it was going to take me a minute to tame it and find something to wear.

I forced myself not to call Clay as he crossed my mind several times wondering what, or who he was with at this moment. I admit silently to how happy I am to have my day mapped out. This will help prevent me from calling him at least for today. And now that Char has finished her work earlier than expected, maybe we can do something after the Spa. I go to my closet, grab my black Vera Wang trousers, white collared

DNKY shirt, and my nine west boots, to wear before I jump in the shower. I decided to just blow dry and bevel my hair, nothing too fancy. I looked at the time; it was almost 9 o'clock. If I leave now; even with traffic, I can be on time. Therefore, I grabbed my Louey V bag and I'm off.

Char and I arrive at the same time as I could see her looking for a space to park and I did the same. I looked for Faizon's truck and didn't see it. I hope she's on her way, or better than that, she's already in the parking lot having trouble finding a spot as well. It would be nice to have a day without the three of us going at it over bullshit, and especially since lately, Char has turned into a domineering, timekeeper. As I continued my hunt for a space, I see that Char has found a spot; she jumps out and is heading towards the Spa. I blow my horn to let her know I'm in the parking lot. She smiles and waves to acknowledge me as she continues her journey into the spa. No doubt to let them know at least two of their three appointments are on time. I finally get lucky as a woman is pulling out. I whip my baby in the vacant space. jump out and head for the door of the Spa. When I get inside, I am surprised to see Faizon's already inside.

"What's up sweetie?"

"Hello." Faizon greets back and stands up to give me a peck on my cheek.

"Where did Char go?"

"She had to pee." Faizon giggled.

"She better get her bladder checked, she stays in the bathroom lately; where's your truck I didn't see it in parking lot?" I inquired.

"Darnell has it, he needed to borrow it to run some errands for his mother today, and since we had plans that would keep us out most of the morning, I didn't mind." Faizon knew that Char and I did not care much for Darnell. We felt he was a sheisty brotha, who always had a gimmick. She must have seen it in my eyes because she immediately included, that he was going to get her truck cleaned and her oil changed, before meeting her back here.

"He's going to be able to do all of that in forty five minutes, because that's how long our session is?" I pressed.

"What's up Lane?" Char asks making her appearance in the reception area. Faizon looked relieved for the welcoming interruption. The receptionist asks us, if we would like something to drink before we get started. We all agreed on green teas, and Sharin the receptionist, walks down the hall to fill our requests. As we waited for Sharin to return with our drinks, we talked about what the plan is after our treatments. Char informs us that she has an important day tomorrow with her firm, and wants to buy a new outfit to represent.

"There is nothing like a new outfit." I concurred.

"What did you have in mind?" Faizon investigated

"I don't know, maybe Neiman Marcus or Anne Taylor."

"Neiman Marcus," Faizon interrupted, "has some new suits I fell in love with last week, but I just brought some belts and a couple pairs of shoes." The silent competition between the two of them at times was hilarious to me, and had to be extremely costly to them. When Faizon's daddy brought her a truck last year, it wasn't a month later Char got the same truck; fully loaded in a different color. Not to mention when Char brought several new clients to her firm, she was rewarded with an all expense paid week off in Italy. Not to be outdone, Faizon had her daddy spring for a week long trip to London. Sharin returns with our green teas, and we sip and talk.

"Char, I'll go with you to Neiman Marcus, I need"... as that word leaves my mouth, I can't help but to smile, "I mean... I want some sweaters, and turtlenecks. I stay cold as hell in that bank."

"What the hell are you smiling about?" Char asked.

"Nothing, I was just thinking about something, someone told me yesterday."

"Ummm humph." She sarcastically replied. We finished our drinks and Sharin had our masseur's greet us up front to walk us to our respective rooms. I followed Boris, as we entered the tranquil room with the peaceful sounds of flowing water being piped in. I get naked, lie on the table, in anticipation to enjoy the next most relaxing 45 minutes Boris my masseur could muster. As Boris massages my legs, I think how I wished it was Clay's hands over my body again. I hope last night was only the beginning, because I have plans for him, if he only allows me the chance. The combination of my night, tea and the serene sounds of the babbling brook, I became so relaxed I dozed off. I don't even know how long I was out before I was jarred out of my sleep hearing Boris softly chanting, my name, "Ms. King, our session is over; if you want more..."

"No, Boris that was great" I didn't realize how tired I was, until I laid on the table.

"That's not a problem Ms. King; I take that as a compliment." I thanked him as he handed me a robe, I got up and gave him a gratuity before he left the room to allow me to get dressed. Faizon and I are dressed, and are now back up front waiting on Char to meet us in the reception area. I watched Faizon as she paces back and forth, looking out the window to see if Darnell has returned with her truck. She is on her cell phone, but it doesn't appear as if she's talking to anyone. Char comes out looking refreshed and looks in the direction of where Faizon is standing. We look at each other and shake our heads, as we're not surprised that Darnell is nowhere to be found. Faizon continues to make calls, while looking out the window. Char and I have had enough and walked up to where Faizon is standing. "Faizon, why not just call him?" I asked, trying not to let on I've been watching her since we had come back to the reception area. "I did, his cell is turned off." I could hear the embarrassment in her voice, so not to make her feel any worse, Char and I decided to leave my car parked at the Spa and take Faizon shopping with us. We would come back later for my car. Faizon agrees after she called Darnell two more times, and he still refused to answer. We got in Char's car, and I was fuming at how disrespectful Darnell is to my girl; I couldn't hold it in any longer, I had let her know how I felt

"Fai, you know I love you, but this shit has got to stop!"

"What's that Lane?" Faizon asks coyly, knowing good and well what I am about to say.

"How you allow Darnell to treat you is bullshit! I don't even know why you go for that shit in the first place, and I know that Char agrees with me." Faizon looks at Char waiting for her to add her two cents, but Char remains quiet until Faizon asks for confirmation.

"Do you feel the same?" Faizon directing her question to Char.

"Yeah, I don't want to call that brother out his name, but that motherfucker is a bum! He half ass works, he is always needing your car, a loan or something to help him with his invisible, ailing mother, you said you've never met."

"Darnell says his mother doesn't like company, she's always feeling too bad." Char and I look at each other in sync.

"Well have you ever talked to her over the phone?" I asked.

"Well no…Darnell says her medication keeps her kind of doped up; it wouldn't make sense to talk to her."

"Darnell seems to have all the answers except how he's going to support himself, and his sickly mother. Men like that make me sick, using their mothers as blankets. Now take Clay and his mothers relationship for instance, he treasures what they have, he even brought her a home and furnished it." I blurted out.

"Who is Clay?" Faizon asked. Char looked at me shook her head and rolled her eyes, translation for I put my foot in my mouth. In an instant, I knew she was right. I opened the gate, and since I did, I might as well open it all the way.

"Clay is the new man in my life."

"Since when?" Faizon snorted, as she scrunched her face up.

"I met him at the game on Friday."

"Wait…. you mean you met someone on Friday, and Char and I are just finding out about it?"

"Well…I knew about it on Friday." Char says softly.

"Oh, I see how y'all bitches do me! Well to hell with y'all."

"Don't be like that," I tell her, "and by the way this is not about me. It's about you, and how you're letting that deadbeat Darnell treat you."

"Don't call him that, he's got a lot on his mind and things aren't going as well for him at the moment."

"Clay's got just as much on his plate, but he handles his business." I said in a bragging tone.

"Look Lane, don't preach to me about some nigga you barely know! He probably just wants some pussy and as soon as he gets it; he's out!" Well, so much for our peaceful day; and no she didn't just go there, now I'm hot. "Look Faizon, you've got what I call, a case of misplaced anger, so please direct that animosity towards the motherfucker who left you stranded in the parking lot of nowhere, with your car. For all you know; he's probably driving some next bitch in it. You better wake up and smell the bullshit homeboy is kicking. You can't call him at home; you've never been to his house; you barely go anywhere together in daylight; he never has any money; what the fuck..? Why can't you ever drive with him to run these fictitious errands for his mother. Darnell got game and you fell for it, hook, line and sinker."

Char had listened to us long enough, and brought us back into focus. "Look y'all two, cut that shit out. We're sistahs and we're not about to let a man, any man, come between us, men come and go. Look at us, will we ever have trouble finding a man? I think not, I keep telling y'all; stop letting men define who you are. You two are worth more than that." I took some cleansing breaths to calm myself down. I don't know what hurt me more, was it that Faizon sided with Darnell, or did she strike a nerve with what she said about Clay just wanting some pussy, because little did she know I had already done the deed. Well, I will soon see as Clay have already had me completely. I know now, I could never let Faizon know that I've already had sex with Clay. "Fai, I apologize, I didn't mean to come at you like that, I just know that you have always been good to Darnell, and I just don't want to see him take advantage of you." Faizon remained silent a few more minutes before letting me know we're good. "I accept Lane, and same here, you're my girl and Char is right, we shouldn't let any man come between us. Plus you're right about something else, I am pissed at Darnell, I know he isn't running errands for his mother." Char gave Faizon a puzzled look through her rearview mirror.

"Well if you know it, why are you allowing him to continue

use you like this?"

"I don't know why...after Max and I broke up; my self esteem hit the floor and I still haven't been able to regain what I allowed Max to take from me." Faizon says, with her eyes welling up with water. I start to feel so guilty for my part in the Darnell issue, and felt it is on me to make her feel better. "Faizon," I started very compassionately. "You are beautiful, inside and out. You don't ever have to settle for just anybody, been there, done that. You have so much to offer the right man, and believe me; there is a good man out there for you. Darnell should be kissing your ass and that is the last thing I'll say about him."

"Lane is right," Char echoes, just don't feel pressured to be with just anyone, the right someone will come and you will know it's him."

We got to Neiman Marcus and just as Faizon said they were having a sale. After we shopped our asses off, we decided to have a nice lunch and get toasted. About midway through my second glass of wine, I got to talking a little more freely than what I wanted to, about my night with Clay. Telling them how he made my body come alive; bragging how he gave me multiple orgasms, and how I cant wait for our next date so I can really throw it on him.

"So... you already gave him the ponanny?" Faizon asks laughing, feeling her wine along with me.

"Yeah he got it, and I was only too glad to give it. Like he said; we're two consenting adults, and I only live once." Faizon stopped me.

"Lane, you don't have to explain your actions to me, just as long as you were both safe, that's all that matters." I took her hand that was resting on the table and patted it for her support of my one night of passion. I was about to tell her how I thought he was a freak, when her phone rang; it's Darnell. I didn't know what he was telling her, but Char and I was shocked when we heard her tell him, to have her truck parked in the parking lot of Spa, in the next half an hour, or she was going to report it stolen. I knew she was pissed because he must have asked her how he was getting home, and her response was `to have his mama pick his ass up`! Char and I cracked the hell up, not caring if he could hear us or not. We were both proud of Faizon's new found independence, and we celebrated with another glass of wine before Char took us to pick up our vehicles. Darnell must have taken Faizon's threat seriously, because her truck was parked just like she told him to. Faizon kissed the both of us, before she got out of Char's vehicle to get in her own. She thanked us for such a therapeutic day, she winked at me and told me keep my legs closed. I laughed and told her "I didn't think so." We waited until she pulled off before Char dropped me off by my car. I grabbed my shopping bags from the trunk and told Char how glad I was to hear that Faizon has kicked that idiot to the curb.

"We'll see. They've been through this before, and he keeps sneaking his way back in." Char says.

"No, I think this time is different, we just need to do more things together on the weekend to keep her mind off him."

"No... that is not the answer," Char rebuts," I don't have time to baby-sit broken hearts, y'all two just have to be able to sniff out who, and what is good for you and what is toxic. Lane, you of all people should know; I know what I'm talking about with the road I had to walk to be able to say that with such clarity."

"Yeah. I do know, and that's why I respect you so much."

"It's not even so much of respecting me, as much as it is respecting and loving yourself. Once you can do that, everything and everybody good will find you. You won't have to look for it, and one more thing; I'm going to do my yoga when I get home in preparation for tomorrow, so I will call you tomorrow."

"In other words; don't call you tonight."

"You said it; I didn't." Char chuckled and adds she loves me before I got in my car and drove off. Just to fuck with her, I called her on her cell as soon as we got to the next light together, just to ask her what's she doing. She called me a crazy bitch and hung up on me. I put on one of my favorite CDs by Kelly Price and took my ass home. It is going on 7 pm and no word from Clay; I don't know how I feel about this since he told me to call him, do I consider this a diss? I needed to find something to do when I got home, at least until 10 o'clock because I knew I wasn't going to call him then. Monday's were my most hectic days, and tomorrow I knew for sure it would be ridiculous. I had some new international accounts involving transfers and tax matters, which always complicated things. Therefore, I knew I must get a good night's sleep to make sure I had my head on tight. I arrived home and pulled out my new purchases; I tried to decide which one of the sweaters I wanted to wear tomorrow, before hanging the rest up. I decided on the black turtleneck, and my grey Chanel suit. Since I was still full from lunch, I made a sandwich; grabbed an iced tea from the fridge, and headed to my room to work on my laptop. I checked my caller ID just to see if maybe he did call. I scrolled down the numbers that did call, but no sign of him calling. However, I noticed my mother did, even better. I would call her back as soon as I got through eating my sandwich. I woofed the sandwich down in a hurry, because I realized I hadn't talked to my parents in two days; which was unusual for me; since my move I talked to them everyday, especially since mommy's been ill. I made that a priority, since I haven't been home since I settled in Atlanta. I took another sip as I hit speed dial for my parents.

"Hello mommy."

"Hi precious, I called you when I got in from church, but you wasn't there."

"I know mommy, I saw your number on my caller ID. I was out."

"Did you go to church today?" My mother asks me in a hopeful voice.

"No, I went to the spa with Char, and Faizon."

"How's Charmine feeling?"

"She's doing well ma." I answered.

"I saw Charmine's ex-fiancé last week in Path- Mark. He was with his new wife...they're expecting a baby in a few months. I didn't know how to respond to that, do I say "fuck that nigga, and his trick ass wife," or be phony as hell and say, "oh that's nice" because I'm talking to my mother. I chose the latter, but abruptly changed the subject.

"Ma, how's daddy?"

"He's fine, he is looking through one of his mechanic books right now. Something is wrong with our alternator, and he wants to see if he can fix it."

"Ma, please tell dad to put that book down, I'm going to wire y'all some money first thing in the morning, so he can take the car in to be looked at. I really wish that dad wouldn't even drive with his eyes getting worse, and worse. I know how crazy people still drive in New York."

"No, I'm not going to tell your dad to put the book down, and no you are not going to send us anymore money. I still have some left over from what you sent me on my birthday a few weeks ago!"

"Mommy; you know I would never disrespect you but; it's my money and I am going to send it in the morning. I just hope you or daddy won't let it sit there, because if it stays in Western Union over twenty four hours someone will steal it." I hated I had to lie to her to get the money but; I knew that was the only way she'd pick it up. See, if my mother didn't know you well, she would automatically classify you as a thief.

"Ma, how are you feeling?"

"I have my good and bad days, and today was a good day, that's why I made it my business to get to church today, and baby that's one of the reasons why I'm calling you, before you heard it from someone else. I could hear the seriousness that was in my mother's voice. "What is it mommy, do you promise me you're doing okay?" I asked; about to break down if she tells me anything other than she is fine.

"Yes baby, I'm fine. It's about Dre." Just hearing his name brought so many emotions, I felt I was going bring my lunch back up. My mind raced as I wondered what happened to him. I knew I had to brace myself for whatever my mother was about to tell me. I swallowed hard, anticipating what my mother will say next. "What happened to Dre?" I asked in the most nonchalant way, I didn't want my mother to know I was about to crumble inside.

"Baby, Sister Johnson told me that he went to jail last night…and that's not it Lane… he's been accused of murder."

"Murder!" I shouted. I hadn't prepare myself well enough to hear this.

"No mommy I don't believe it! Dre is a lot of things, but he's not a murderer." I can't seem to help the steady flow of tears rolling down my face. My mother tried to comfort me with her words and voice, as she's always done in the past when she knew I was hurting.

"Don't cry baby, I knew you was going feel this way, that's why I wanted to be the one to tell you."

"I'm glad you did mommy, it helps me a lot to hear it from you." I said now sobbing loudly.

"Well baby, I hate you had to hear it at all." I knew I could not stay on the phone another minute because I literally felt sick.

"Mommy, I'm happy to hear that you and daddy are doing well, and don't forget to tell daddy to pick up the money first thing tomorrow, but I have to hang up now."

"Listen Lane, I wish that I was there with you, but I'm not, so remember what you was taught; God is always by your side and HE will be at Dre's side too, if he didn't do what they are saying he did. I love you sweetheart. Have a good night."

"I love you too mommy, and kiss daddy for me, I'll talk to you tomorrow when I get in from work." As soon as I hung up the phone, the floodgates opened. I knew what Char said but I've got to call her. I dialed her number, barely able to read the numbers, as my eyes are filled with tears. Char picked up about to read me my rights.

"Hello Lane, didn't I"...

"Charrrr," I cried out.

"Lane, what's the matter, what going on?" I'm crying so hard, I could barely get my words out.

"I just got through talking to mom."

"What's wrong with ma?" Char asks in hysteria.

"No. It's Dre!" I stammered.

"Wait Lane, calm down, what's happened to him?" I tried to suppress my sobs and get the whole story out without crying uncontrollably. Char patiently waited me out, long enough to pull myself together, until I finally felt that I was able to get out a few sentences without choking. "Char," I start slowly, "I just got through talking to ma." Before I proceed with the rest, I took a few more breaths. When I felt that helped some, I finished telling her about how my mother's church sister told her of Dre's misfortune.

"Oh my God Lane, are they sure?"

"I don't know, he was only arrested last night. I don't know who I could even call to ask about this. You know his mother hasn't been around ever since she became a crack head, and he never knew his daddy." I added.

"Lane, I know this may sound like I'm adding fuel to the fire, but what about his girlfriend?"

"What about her Char; do you really expect me to call the bitch that fucked our relationship up in the first place!?"

"Look Lane, I know that may have sounded insensitive, but if you want to know what's really going on with him, you may have to call someone who knows first hand." I knew what Char was saying is correct, but I didn't feel I could call her and be civil.

"Alright Char, I'll figure something out. I'll talk to you tomorrow."

"Are you going to be okay, because I can come over?"

"No Char, I'm fine."

"Liar."

"Okay. I'm not fine, but I know we both have a busy day tomorrow, and neither of us, can afford to be half-cocked."

"Okay sweetie, I love you. Call me if you need me."

"Good night Char."

"Goodnight Lane." Char must've known I was in pain; normally she wouldn't even have allowed me to entertain her on anything concerning Dre. And she was willing to come and spend the night, and hear me cry on her shoulder all night about Dre. Yeah- she knew I was hurting. Well, so much for having a good start to the good week. I tossed, and turned all night; each time I looked at the time, maybe only thirty minutes or so have passed. I knew this was going be a long, miserable night. After my fifth glass of water I decide to just get up. I'm not fooling myself; its no way I was going to get a good night's sleep. Who could I call about this to get some information without resorting to Renee? I bust my brain trying to figure out what is that dude's name, Dre use to bring to the house all the time, trying to fuck me behind Dre's back. What is his name?

After wrecking my brain, to the point of a headache, I've finally come to the realization that Char might be right, I may have to call that bitch after all. And the last time I saw her, her legs was in the air of my bed and she had the nerve to want to fight me in my house over Dre. A surge of anger shot through my body just remembering that night, now look what's happened, karma is a motherfucker. I returned to my room and decided I will continue my quest in the morning. My alarm goes off 5 o'clock sharp, and I am still sleepy as hell. I showered, put my hair in a neat bun, and got dressed for my chaotic day. I looked in the mirror and thought how stressed I looked. Who would ever believe I had a day at the spa just yesterday? I don't have time to even think, I have to be at work with my game face on in one hour.

Just as I anticipated, my International client had several overseas accounts. He wanted to transfer funds over the amount that would have allowed him legally not to involve Uncle Sammy, but since he did, I had to be extremely thorough. The paperwork was always the most grueling part of the process for me on a normal day, let alone the day after I found out that the man who I was madly in love with, has been arrested for murder. The process would have not been so lengthy, if Mr Akoyeiu had not flirted with me the entire time; this is too much for me to handle today.

Thank God, Mr Akoyeiu will soon complete his paper signing so I can get some air before I pass out. Mr Akoyeiu thanked me, and the bank for the services he'd been rendered as he signed his last few papers. I informed him that he has immediate access to his funds, and shook his hand as I walked him to the door. He turned to ask me one last time, would I like to have dinner with him tonight. Dinner! I've just been hit by a train, and you want me to have fucking dinner with you, is what I wanted to say, but instead I told Mr Akoyeiu that I was flattered by his invitation, but it was against our bank's policy. This didn't mean shit to him as he slipped me his card and hotel room information. As soon as he was out of sight, I grabbed my bag, and sprinted to my car; I just needed some air and coffee to stop my jitters. I walked to my car and the closer I got, I saw what looked like a rose and an envelope on my windshield. What is going on; it must have been placed there by mistake. No; I saw correctly, it was a rose and a card attached, I snatched the card off my windshield and opened it.

Lane,
Thank you for a memorable night,
Clay.

How did he know where... that's right; I gave him my

business card, it has all my work details on it. Boy, he is just what I needed, I inhaled the rose and allowed the fragrance to fill my head with thoughts as lovely as the rose left for me. I slumped my body onto the soft leather in my car, just thinking about my next step. Do I call Clay, or Dre's girlfriend Renee? I wanted to find out as much as I could; I just didn't want to call her. Who else could I call? It took me- what I felt was all morning to remember the name of Dre's friend. I only knew his nickname, but finally it hit me, Cash; his name is Cash, but that would be paradise for him. He may even try to pick up where he left off by asking me to get with him. I decided to call Clay instead and thank him for my rose. I looked at my watch, it was only a little after lunchtime. That left me to wonder, what time did he leave the note and rose. I smiled to myself at how thoughtful his gesture was. I got his card out and dialed his number.

"Hello, this is Clay."

"Hello Clay, this is Lane."

"How are you, did you find my note?"

"Yes, and the rose. That's why I'm calling to say thank you."

"I asked you to call me yesterday."

"Yes you did." I find myself smiling at his forceful clamor.

"So you mean, if I hadn't left the note, you wasn't going to call, I can see you're gonna be hardheaded." We both started to laugh.

"I was going to call you, but my day took a couple of bad turns."

"Is you mother alright?"

"Yes she is fine; I spoke to her yesterday. That's sweet of you to ask."

"My point is, if your peoples are good, then everything else is trivial." He says putting the seriousness back in his voice, and putting things in perspective for me.

"You're right. I just had a bad day, and I didn't want to call you; when I was in that kind of mood."

"How about next time you let me be the judge of what I want. Alright?" I said yes to him like I did when I was a child answering my daddy.

"I'm glad you're good, I just want to let you know; I'm feeling you Lane. I meant it when I said I want to see more of you."

"After Saturday night, I don't think there's anymore of me to see." I teased.

"Oh… I see you got jokes, but I think there's a whole lot more of you to see. How about Friday night?" I kept repeating Friday in my head, to jar if I had made plans with the girls.

"I'm free on Friday."

"That's good, the only thing; it has to be a late one. I fly out to Philly on some business tomorrow and I return on Friday. My flight lands after 10pm, if that's too late just let me know."

"No that's fine, I don't have a curfew." I said jokingly.

"Good, I'll call you from the plane, I'll take it from there."

"Okay, Clay, see you then and have a safe flight."

"I will. Bless." He's gone. I sat in my car a while longer, and pondered why did I want to waste time on finding out about Dre. Clearly Clay can be a fresh start for me, and more than that, I'm feeling the brother too; and a lot. I went for my much needed caffeine and head back to my office. How can I outdo Saturday when I see Clay on Friday. He'll probably expect me to have sex with him, and so what if he does the first time is always the most awkward and since we got that out of the way, everything else should be natural. After the brief phone conversation I had with Clay, I made the decision not to call Renee. In retrospect, I was in a relationship with Dre, and he chose not to be in a relationship with me. I had to let him go as difficult as that may be, because the truth of the matter is I still loved him.

Relay-tionships

Chapter Five

The days felt like they were in snail mode, I was so anxious to see Clay I kept myself busy enough not to miss him so badly, although I thought about him everyday. I definitely made sure I stayed busy enough not to call Renee, concerning Dre. Char and Faizon played a big part in that. Faizon was busy trying to promote her new fashion line, and on days that I wasn't too stressed from work, she would ask me to help her. Faizon was used to getting everything she asked for. Her dad owned several car dealerships, which was doing extremely well, so Faizon never really had to lift a finger to do anything. Her fashion line was the first thing she's ever attempted to do on her own, and even when her dad offered his help she declined.

I was proud of her, seeing her transcend into adulthood. Darnell kept calling her trying to finagle his way back into her heart, but she held strong and refused to relive that part of her life. Char called that night before I went to bed to ask if I heard anything more about Dre. I told her I hadn't and my mother's decision against offering me any more information about him, when she realized how much I still cared for him. Char was happy to learn of my mother's decision and said she was going treat Faizon and me to dinner on Thursday after work; and for us to meet on Piedmont Ave. She said her boss had taken her to this new restaurant there, and she liked it so much she wanted to take us. I was looking forward to that because the next day would be Friday and Clay would be home. That night I dreamt that Dre and met Clay, and Dre killed him. This whole murder situation with Dre was getting to me; did he do it, was I living with a murderer? I was baffled by the uncertainty, I was so sure that Dre would have never cheated on me, but not only did he cheat on me, he brought her into our bed, so go figure. Today was a much better day; I finished work early and headed towards Piedmont when my cell rings and its Clay.

"What's up baby?"

"What's up with you sir, are you back in Atlanta?"

"No, I'm still in Philly, missing you."

"Oh, how sweet is that!"

"Nah, but I mean it; I can't wait to get home. I had a mad dream about you last night." Oh, shit, what a coincidence, but I can't tell him I dreamed that my ex killed him. I quickly covered up my silence by asking Clay what he dreamed about. All I could hear was him laughing.

"Oh, it must've been a good dream, to make you laugh like that."

"Oohh yeah, it was a good dream."

"Tell me, I have to hear this."

"I'll put it to you like this, I want you wear that same color lipstick you had on the last time I saw you." I knew it, that Fashion Fare will do it all the time, but I continue to act like I didn't have a clue what he was getting at.

"What lipstick, and why are you dreaming about my lipstick?" I laughed nervously.

"I'll tell you when I see you."

"You better."

"What are you doing tonight?"

"Char is taking me and our other friend to dinner at some restaurant she tried last week with her boss."

"Alright then, enjoy yourself and I'll see you tomorrow."

"I can't wait, and uumm…. stop dreaming about lipstick." I told him smirking.

"Stop wearing that sexy ass lipstick; on your sexy ass lips, you make a grown man want to do some things." He left me feeling so good with what he told me, I made the decision right then that if he wanted to make love tomorrow night, we would. That evening, I approached the restaurant to see that Char is already there and is on the phone. No doubt with Faizon telling her she was going to be late, because she broke a nail or something but the closer I get I can see the look of horror on Char's face. I got so freaked; I parked in a handicapped space and jumped out. I rushed over to Char to hear her ask the person on the other end, is she going to make it. Char looks up to discover me standing there; she takes my hand while still on the phone and starts to drag me wildly to her car. I jerk gently on her hand for her to let me in on what is going on. Char is ending the conversation with, "Okay Mrs Hill, Lane and I, are on our way." Mrs Hill is Faizon's mother, and why aren't we waiting for Faizon? I ask myself these questions, but not much longer before Char hangs up and screams.

"That bastard!"

"Who are you talking about and where is Faizon?" Char

looks at me with tears in her eyes and tells me that Darnell had beat Faizon half to death, and she is in Piedmont hospital. "He did what?" Her mouth was moving, but she's not making any sense, or was I just in a state of shock, what more would happen this week. Char tells me we have to get to her in a hurry. I can see the parking attendant looking for a handicap decal in my car, so I tell Char to lets take my car. We jumped in and I broke every speed limit to get to the hospital. We get to the hospital, and asked for information. The desk clerk, types in her name, looks back up at us, and asks are we family?

"Hell yeah" I snap, shouting at the receptionist.

"Ma'am, calm down its hospital policy that I ask."

"I could care less about policy, what room is my sister in?"

"Ms. Hill is in ICU."

"ICU" Char and I both say in unisonant and hauled ass towards the elevator. As we reach the ICU unit we see Mr and Mrs Hill standing outside her room, Mrs Hill has her face buried in Mr Hill's chest. Char and I walk slowly towards them as to not intrude on their privacy. Mr Hill looks in our direction and notices us, his eyes beet red from crying and rage, motions for us to come over. Mrs Hill becomes aware of our presence and walks to us with her legs wobbling. Char takes her hands, to prevent her from falling in the corridor. She looked like she really needed someone to get her a chair. "How is she, what happened?" I asked in a panic, all of the things we really needed to know. Mr Hill walked our way, and gestured for us to follow him into the waiting room. Char and I continued to cushion Mrs Hill in between us, while Mr Hill loosened his tie, before he started to fill us in. He sat directly across from us on the smaller waiting room sofa, his tone was almost in a growl he is so angry. "I got a call from Faizon's neighbor, telling me that she had to call 911 to Faizon's house, after being awakened to screams and shouting.

His voice got even raspier as he continued the story. He went on to tell us that the neighbor had seen Darnell running out of the house holding something in his hands. She remembered that just earlier during the week Faizon had told her that she had broke it off with him. Faizon's neighbor thought she had better go check on her. He concluded with how glad he was she did take the time to check on his baby. "That bastard had beaten her in the head with some kind of stick; she couldn't get his plate number because when she went back out he had already slipped the security gates. Thank God, the neighbor is a nurse, and started to treat her before the police and ambulance even got there."

As Mr Hill recapped the story, Mrs Hill cried uncontrollably. Char and I tried to console her but we knew that was going to be impossible, Faizon was their one and only "Princess." I felt horrible for Faizon, and her parents. I wanted to release my own tears that I'd been choking back, since I heard of this ordeal but the last thing I wanted to do was to upset the Hill's even more. Distraught; I couldn't help but think of the two losers that Faizon and I got hooked up with. I looked at Mr Hill who has always been a tall, strong, no nonsense kind of guy, but today; looked small and weak. I asked him did the police arrest Darnell yet. He answered in a vicious snarl, that they'd better get him before he does, and I knew by the way he said it; he meant every word. Char went into her shut down mode, speaking only when she was spoken to, and her answers were always short and sweet. We sat in the waiting room for what seemed like a hundred years, until Faizon's team of doctors came in and wanted to speak to the Hill's privately.

Char and I excused ourselves and told the Hills we were

headed to the hospital Cafeteria, and would return shortly. They nodded and returned their focus back to the doctors. I looked at Char and knew I couldn't hold my tears back anymore, that's our best friend and she could be dying from the hands of someone we hate from the second she introduced him to us. Through my tears, I managed to tell Char that I wished Mr Hill did get to him before the police did. Mr Hill would impose a far better justice for Faizon than the police ever could. "I can't believe it, Lane, that motherfucker has lost his mind. I hated Faizon doesn't have any brothers" Char is telling me, her hands shaking so badly I thought she would spill her coffee.

"I want to know how he got into her house, what caused him to snap?"

"I know what caused him to snap, he saw how well Faizon was doing with her fashion line, and he couldn't bear the fact she was moving on without him."

"I'll take it a step further, that imp saw dollar signs and you know he didn't want to let go of that." Char alludes.

"I pray he got someone to look after his sickly ass mother, because his ass is going to jail." I added very sarcastically. I take a couple more sips of my coffee, when I see Mr Hill walking over to us; he looks taller, even stronger and got his swagger back. He sits down, and I notice his voice isn't cracking anymore.

"How is she, is everything alright?" I asked. Char eyes got bigger than I've ever seen them.

"Thank God, she is going to be fine, and I'm so grateful for the quick response from her neighbor. There are no signs of brain damage, the doctor told us if her vitals signs remain strong she will be out of ICU in twenty-four hours; the doctors just want to keep an eye on her to make sure she continues to make progress. I do want to ask you a question though; I hope you two won't feel like you are betraying her trust." I looked at Char, puzzled at what he would want to know that could possibly betray our trust with Fazion. I tell him sure; to ask away. We want to help in any way we can, especially if it's to keep Darnell away from Faizon the rest of her life. "Did Princess ever tell you she is...I mean... was pregnant?" I knew Princess is the nickname he has for Faizon, but I wanted him to repeat what he just said, because it sounded as if he said she is...was pregnant. "No." I said quickly. Char shook her head no so fast I thought she was going to give herself a nose bleed.

"Well the doctor said Faizon would be fine but due to the trauma, the fetus did not survive, it was about five weeks old and I feel I can be honest with you two since I consider y'all like my daughters as well... I'm glad she lost the baby. I hated Darnell from the beginning, and I don't ever want him in my Princess life again. I know a baby would have complicated things, and knowing Princess; she would never begrudge her baby of seeing him!" He pauses, and looks as if the next thing out of his mouth will be painful to say, but he continues just the same. "I will ask one thing, and that is you keep what I just told you about the baby to yourselves. I don't want Mrs Hill or Princess to ever find out how I feel, but I had to release it and get it out of my system."

I placed my hand on his left shoulder and gently rubbed it and told him he never has to worry about that, because I feel the same way. Char seconds the motion. "I only hope when she gets home; she'll just let me take care of her." Mr Hill says pathetically, I think he already knows she is not going to allow that to happen, but I tried to offer him some hope by saying, "Maybe she will."

We asked if we could see her before we left, but Mr Hill

sways us against it, he knew we couldn't handle seeing the trauma that caused to her head ,and asked us to wait until at least she's out of ICU. He added he wished that he, and especially Mrs Hill never had to see her like that. He asked us for one last favor, and that was to take Mrs Hill home; we agreed without thinking twice. We gulped down our coffee and headed back up to the ICU floor. Mrs Hill was still standing at Faizon's room window watching the doctor's work on Faizon. Mr Hill walked up to her, rubbed her back and kisseed her lovingly on her cheek. He told her we're going to take her home. Mrs Hill looks at us and speaks very softly to her husband. "Roger, you know I am not leaving our baby, as long as she stays in this hospital, so will I." Mr Hill didn't try and persuade her any further, he knew she wasn't going anywhere, he just thought he'd give it a try. "Well ladies," Mr Hill looked at us and said, "My wife has spoken." We kissed the both of them, and told them if they needed anything, no matter what time it is to give us a call.

The Hills agreed and thanked us for loving their Princess so much. As I was talking to Faizon's parents, Char was busy writing down numbers to give to both of them in case they did need us. After Char passed out the numbers, we headed towards the elevator. Char and I were both so drained from the horrific ordeal we postponed our dinner date. Char asked me would I oppose if she invited herself to my house for an overnight visit. "I was hoping you would say that." I pepped up with the thought of having company on a night such as this. I told her I just bought a new bottle of wine; and we could order pizza in. I reminded her that we needed to go back for her car and then we can head home. Char explained, she felt so tense from has happened to Faizon, she asked if it would be okay if I drove her back later before the restaurant closes to pick up her car. She was in no mood to drive right now. She just wanted to relax a little. I told her that was fine with me, but asked if she felt safe with leaving her truck there for that long. She assured me that the restaurant stayed so busy, they wouldn't even know the difference and we would be back long before they closed, so it shouldn't matter.

The drive to my house was dreary. I'm still fuming with the thought of how that motherfucker entered Faizon's house and violated her. Now she has to deal with the fact that she has lost her baby. I had to ask Char did she think Faizon knew about the pregnancy.

"Char, do you think Faizon was aware that she was carrying Darnell's child."

"That's hard to answer Lane for two reasons. First, she probably knew we would try to persuade her to think long and hard if she was sure a baby by Darnell was something she really wanted to consider. Second; she has been so busy trying to promote her fashion line she may have already made up mind on what she wanted to do and didn't want us to know of her decision."

"You're right, that is hard to say, I hate she had to be alone with him. I wonder did he know?"

"Who gives a flying fuck about what he knew. I just want him to know he is in a world of trouble; he has fucked over the right somebody's daughter now. Char was so on point with that it broke the ice. I had to laugh thinking about what Mr Hill said about the police better catch him before he does. I joked with Char about how serious he was when he said it, Char had to laugh too. In fact, Char went a step further imitating how Mr Hill's face screwed up when he was talking about Darnell.

Approaching my house, I told Char to call 411 to get the number to Pizza House so we can order from the car, so by the time we reached my house; our order should be on its way. Char obliges, and orders two medium veggies, breadsticks, and something gooey for our dessert. Ten minutes later we're at my front door, I start to undress at the door; I kicked off my shoes and started to strip from my work clothes.

Char asked me for some sweats, and a tee shirt so she could do the same.

"Where's that bottle of wine you keep bragging about!" Char hollers to me from the kitchen as I continue to unwind from the day in my room.

"Look in the wine cabinet; doh-doh." I yell back at her, "Throw on some Biggie while you're at it, I need to release some of this stress I have." I continued.

"How about we put on some Gato or Norman Brown, Biggie is the last thing you need to hear." I quickly remind Char whose house she's in.

"Char, there is a time for Gato and Norman; and then there is a time for Biggie, and this is the time for some Biggie. I want to dedicate a song to Darnell."

"A song to Darnell?"

"Yeah…Ready to die."

"Girl you are so crazy."

"Yeah, so I've been told." I listened to my messages, nothing of importance, so I head for the living room to join Char, where she is trying to pretend she can't find my Biggie CD. I walked over to my CD caddy, looked in the B section and pulled out B.I.G and tossed it to Char, "I burst your bubble didn't I?" I teased her. Before she could respond; my doorbell rings and it's the delivery man with our pizza. While I fumbled with my stereo, I told Char to grab my bag and pay the man. Char tells me it's her treat; she was planning to take us to dinner anyway. She pays the deliveryman, and he leaves. I blasted Biggie and danced by myself in the kitchen, while I fixed a quick salad and poured me a glass of wine.

"Listen…I am not going to be listening to that shit all night. I had a rough day and the last thing I want to hear is drug dealers rapping about guns, money, ho's, and… more, guns, money and ho's, don't they got tired of the same ole shit. I thought you were just going through a phase in college, I didn't know you would still be rapping in your thirties."

"Listen Ms. Prissy, the world is based on guns, money, and whores and you want to condemn the messenger, if it makes you happy you can listen to Norman after I hear Biggie."

"Good, cause I don't want to have to pack up my shit, and start walking to get my truck."

"Stop fronting…you know your ass is not walking anywhere." Char smirks because she knew I was telling the truth. I grabbed my wine and danced, and rapped right along with Biggie.

"Girl how in the hell do you remember every line to those songs, if that's what you want to call them."

"You're sounding like Clay now, he was shocked to hear that I loved rap, you know even if I didn't love rap, I'd have to learn… being the wife of the CEO of a record company, I better know his product." I said, and took a long sip of from my glass.

"You better drink up; there you go talking crazy again."

"Nah. I was just joking about that but, on a serious note, Clay's coming home tomorrow, and we have a late night planned, but with what happened to Faizon today I felt it would be inappropriate for me to keep it."

"No Lane, don't feel like that. This may sound harsh, but

life goes on. I have plans for tomorrow as well, and I'm going to keep them."

"With who?"

"Nothing major, I just made plans with my boss."

"You've been getting real chummy, chummy with your boss lately."

"It's nothing like that, he just appreciates my hard work, and dedication and he just wants to show me how much."

"Yeah, that's what I'm afraid of, but how much he wants to show you is the question." Giving her a contemptuous look.

"You nasty, and get your mind out of the gutter Lane, everything isn't always about sex."

"Oh really…well what is it about if not sex. Don't think Mr Boss man don't want to hit it, because he does; and the moment you let your guard down, you two will be fucking like two champion horses."

"You got it all wrong Lane, my boss is white."

"So fucking what, you're a beautiful woman and that's all he sees at the moment, what… because he's white he can't find you desirable? Plus you said yourself, Mr Martin looks like David Beckham, shit I'd fuck David Beckham."

"Okay, you're right about that, but I don't think he even sees me in that way."

"Char… you are a smart, classy, gorgeous creature. Not to mention those tight ass skirts you be wearing. Think about how many women come on to you when we're out, you don't think he sees you as beautiful because you are African American….to be so intelligent, you are sounding really silly right now."

"Nah I just never thought of it like that…but to be honest;

if he wanted to have a relationship outside of work, I would."

"Char again and I repeat, you're sounding really stupid. Aren't you the one who's always preaching to me and Faizon about being with men who will treat us well, and respect us not just for the pussy…so it shouldn't matter if Mr Martin is a dark purple, or green, if he treats you well; which it sounds like he does it shouldn't matter. Your only concern should be is that he is your boss and you don't want to fuck around and muddle business with pleasure."

"Now you're talking to me like I'm stupid, everything we've done up to this point have always been on a professional level, he has never crossed any boundaries, and neither have I!"

"Look, I'm not saying that you two haven't been professional, I'm just saying don't get the roles confused."

"I won't…, let's eat our pizza, it's getting cold." I had a feeling that Char wasn't being totally honest with me or herself about her true feelings for Mr Martin but that was not for me to say. I haven't always been the best judge in my own relationships, so I damn sure shouldn't be giving out any lovers advice. After Biggie, I kept my promise and let Char listen to Norman Brown. We continued to talk about Faizon, Darnell, Dre and Kamel. The trip down memory lane must have gotten to deep for her, because Char ended it all of a sudden when thinking about Kamel; and how they split up. I knew she had to be devastated.

That day was almost perfect, she looked beautiful in her designer gown, and flowers costing as much as a car. Like I said almost perfect; until he decided not to show because he, "just couldn't do it," but I've always admired how she came out of that.

"Lane before we get to deep in our flashback shit, take me to get my car." Now I'm mad at myself and Char, that we just didn't pick up car before I came home.

"Char... do we...

"Yes, we do. That's why I asked your ass, before we even left the parking lot of the hospital, would you take me back to get my truck and you said yes, so get off your lazy ass and take me to get my truck!"

"Ummm. I believe my mother is still in Brooklyn, and she is the only woman who can order me around!"

"Get your ass up, so we can get back, I'm sleepy as shit now. I threw on my sneakers and we headed back to the restaurant to pick up Char's truck. No sooner than we get in my car, Char is snoring. I didn't realize how sleepy I was either until I started driving. I had to open my window to keep me from dozing off myself. So many thoughts crossed my mind, Faizon, Clay, and I just remembered I did not call my mother. I'll call her as soon as I step back in the door; I know she's waiting for my call.

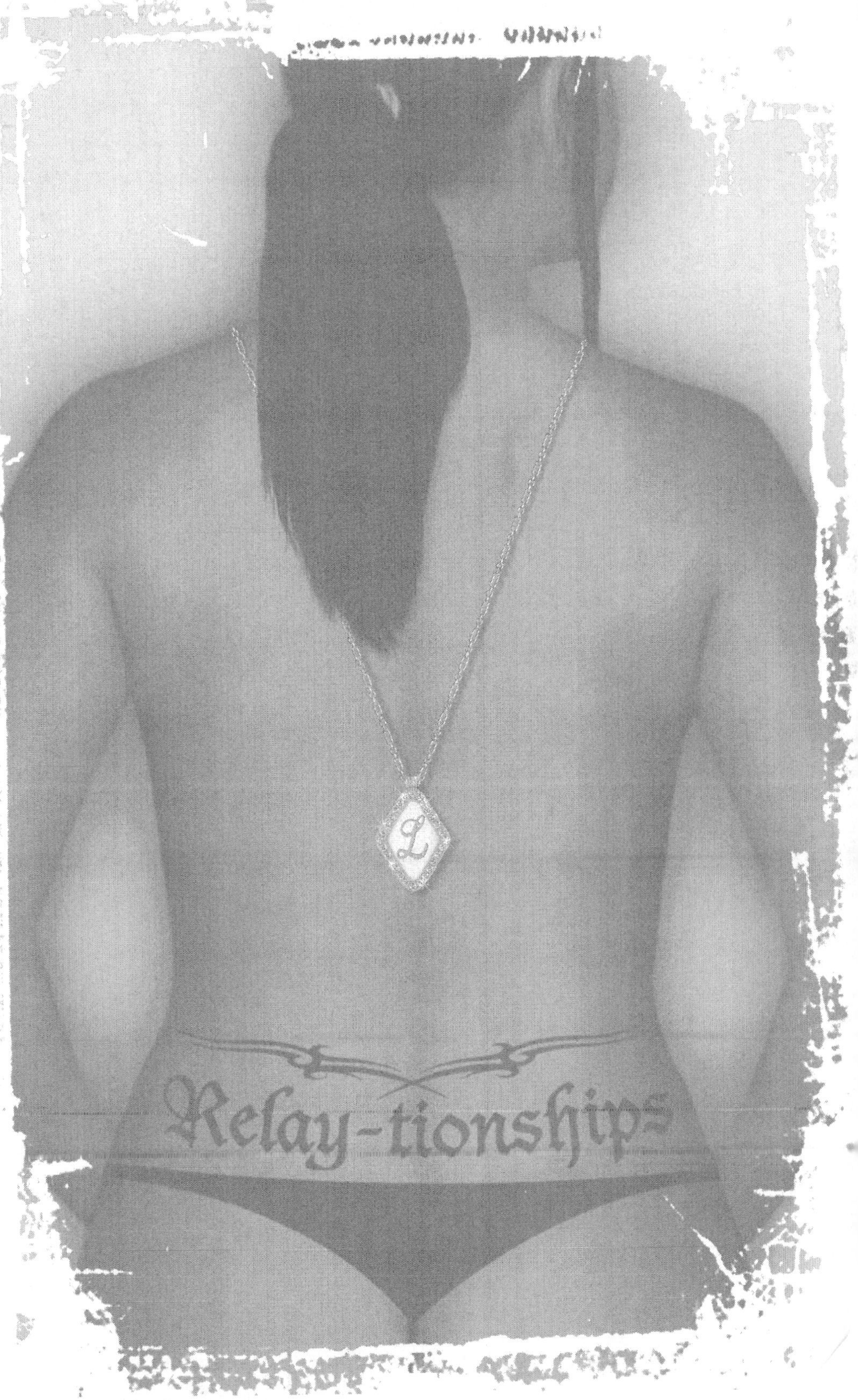
L
Relay-tionships

102

Chapter Six

I can't wait to see Clay tomorrow; I'm going to tease the hell out of him with my lipstick. I need to buy some strawberries, and have them dipped in chocolate for temptation. As we near the restaurant, I wake Char so she can get her mind right before she takes the wheel. After the day we just had I don't know what I would do if something happened to her while driving. "Wake up Char, we're almost there, let your window down to get some fresh air." She is still a little groggy, but complies.

"Char, do you want me to stop at the store so you can get a red bull or something?"

"No, I'm good; I'll just take it slow. I didn't think I was this tired."

"What did you expect? Our day hasn't been the greatest and before you know it, its morning, and we start all over." I couldn't believe that the restaurant was still packed.

"I told you this is the hottest place in Atlanta right now, as soon as Faizon gets better, I'm still going to bring you two here.

"Yeah, I hope so; this spot looks really nice."

"It is; when Anthony....I mean Mr Martin brought me here, we had a very nice time."

"Yeah, you said it right the first time; Anthony, you don't have to front for me, I know what's going on."

"Really..., then please tell me?" Charmine insists while giving me this crazy grin.

"I will say this then you can get out of my car, get in yours, and I'll see you back at the house. You're only hurting yourself, trying to convince yourself you don't have feelings for Anthony...Oh, I mean Mr Martin." I said in a snide tone, "now scam, I'll see you at the house."

"Shut up Lame!"

"I told you about that." I put my baby in drive, and sped off leaving Char in the parking lot. I got home before Char and start clearing the dishes we had from dinner. Char pulled up before I even closed the dishwasher door. I let her in and grabbed the phone to call my mother before it got too late.

"Hi mommy, how are you doing today?"

"Well to be honest with you baby, today wasn't such a great day for me."

"What's the matter; are you sick?"

"Just a little sick, I think I ate something that didn't agree with me."

"Ma, I called your doctor last week and he told me that he talked to you about your poor eating habits, and I'm going to need you to follow his instructions, you know if you need me to come home, all you have to do is say the word and I'm there."

"I know that baby, I'm sure it was just the catfish, but I will

104

do better about what I eat, no need to worry so much about me." Too late, I'm worried sick about my mother and know, that I have to plan a trip home as soon as possible. I try to camouflage my feelings and ask about my dad, before my mom catches on.

"How's daddy?"

"Ooohh, he's fine; his only problem is he's stubborn as all get out."

"It sounds like the both of you are having the same problem with stubbornness. My mother always laughs at me when she feels I am being too parental. "How was your day baby?" I lied and told her fine, it made no sense for me to upset her with the news about Faizon, I will tell her when both of them are doing a little better. "Well ma, I had a busy day, but I wanted to make sure I did call you before you and daddy went to bed, tell daddy I love him, and kiss him for me." Char yells out for me to say hello to the both of them.

"Oh, ma; Char says hello to you, and daddy."

"Hey Charmine." My mother answers, as if she could hear her. "Char, ma says hello. Okay ma I will talk to you tomorrow before I leave work, I love you."

"I love you too baby and talk to you tomorrow. I hung up the phone and went back up front with Char where she is reading a magazine.

" I'm surprised I didn't hear you ask about Dre."

"What... are you eavesdropping on my conversation with my mother now?"

"Now why would I have to eavesdrop, I just thought it was weird you had to talk to your mother in your bedroom."

"There's nothing weird about it, I was getting my clothes out for tomorrow while on the phone; that's called multi–tasking."

"Don't be funny…don't forget in college it was me who taught you the art of multi-tasking."

"You wish, and on that note I'm going to bed. See you dopey; you know where to find extra bedding."

"See you sleepy." I couldn't wait for the night to be over, so I could see my baby Clay tomorrow. I forgot what time he said his flight landed, it doesn't matter it's not like I'm not going to wait for him whatever time he gets in, but I think he said ten. Good, that gives me plenty of time to do what I need to do. I will want to check on Faizon and the Hill's. After talking with my mother tonight, I will be placing a call to her doctor, just to make sure everything is alright with her. My alarm went off and Char is already up and dressed, when I head for the kitchen to get a cup of coffee.

"Good morning Lane,"

"Good morning… damn it!"

"What happened?"

"I forgot to turn the timer to the coffee maker on."

"Girl get a grip, so it'll take you a few extra minutes to make a cup of Joe…it's not that serious."

"I know it's not that serious Char. I just don't like wasting time in the morning; you know I'm not a morning person!"

"Who is?"

"You're up mighty early, didn't you sleep well?"

"Yeah actually, I slept like a baby it's just that I have so much I need to do today, you know I'm going to Piedmont to check in on Faizon, and see how the Hill's are holding up."

"Once again, you and I are on that mental telepathy shit, I made plans to do the same thing. What time were you planning to head to the hospital?"

"About nine, I have a few late appointments and Mr Martin and I have plans."

"I was hoping that I could meet you, but I know I can't make it at nine. I have a meeting at that time, so call me after you see her if they let you in so I'll know what has changed, if anything."

"Will do …thanks for the sleepover. What time is your date with Clay?"

"I don't know exactly, his plane lands at ten; so I know it will be any time after that."

"Alright then, I'll call you when I see Faizon, if they are letting non relatives in."

"Alright sweetie, I'll wait for your call. Have a good day with Anthony."

"Don't be fresh, you mean Mr Martin."

"Don't you be fresh; I said exactly what I meant to say." Char gave me a sinister smile and slams my door on her way out. My day was already compiled with things I didn't want to deal with before Clay's arrival. I knew I had to go and see Faizon, but I really wasn't looking forward to it. Who really wants to see their best friend in the state her dad said she was in physically. Knowing that once she recovered from the physical scars, the real work would kick in. We would have to deal with the psychological scars this was going to leave behind with the loss of the baby and all. I did know that Char and I would be there for her.

I drank a strong cup of coffee and thought about how glad I would be to see Clay. I gulped the last few sips of coffee and hit the shower. While I'm in the shower my thoughts are with Clay again, I take my soapy cloth and caress my pussy with the attention I knew Clay would give me tonight. I let out a sigh with just the thought of his touch. I quickly tried to think of something else to get focused; I didn't have time today to daydream. I jumped out of the shower, and rushed to get dressed to beat that ridiculous Friday traffic. Disgusted, I sat behind a mound of eighteen wheelers, I laugh at myself to even think I would be traffic free. I'm about to get very frustrated at this rude trucker when my cell rings. It's Clay and all of a sudden all is forgiven with the trucker.

"Good morning Clay, I'm so glad to hear your voice."

"Good morning baby, what's up?"

"Well a lot since we last spoke."

"What's going on?" Clay asks in a concerned manner.

"For one, my best friends ex nearly beat her to death but succeeded in killing their unborn child."

"Damn, are you talking about Charmine."

"No…it's my other girlfriend, her name is Faizon. I met her when I first moved here and started working at the bank, she would always bring her dad's deposits in the bank for him, and we formed a relationship from then."

"Did they catch dude?"

"That I don't know, but I hope they do…he has to pay for what he did."

"No doubt, do you want to cancel tonight, because if you do I'll understand?" How in the heck do I say aloud, that I'd rather spend my time fucking the shit out of you, than to see my best friend.

"No Clay, I made plans to adjust my day accordingly to see her, plus her parents said they would keep me posted of any changes."

"Alright…. that sounds cool, but if you change your mind don't' hesitate." Is he backing out of the date, he seems a little too eager to accommodate.

"Clay….did you need to postpone tonight?"

"No," he answers sharply, which was a good sign and then he continues. "I just know the need for women to be there for each other; don't forget I told you about growing up around all women. I don't care how strong y'all say y'all are; you still have the need to lean on your girls." I start to giggle as if I was a teenager again and told him he was right.

"The reason I'm calling you so early is because I got an earlier flight and I wanted to see if I had you meet me at my house, would that put you out of your way this way I can see you sooner."

"That sounds good; I just need your address."

"As soon as we finish talking I'll have my assistant call you with everything you need to know. One more thing… I don't want to be too presumptuous but I have to ask…"

"What is it Clay?

"Do you have anymore black lace?" He lets out this sly chuckle

"Why?"

"Like I said, I don't want to seem like that's all I want, but I must be truthful with you. I can't seem to get you out of my head standing there in that black, and tonight you'll be on my turf so… I was just wondering if you had some more of that sexy shit. That would really give me something to come home to." I hesitated in giving my answer. I didn't want him to think I only wanted to be his fuck buddy. I did want him tonight; in fact, I have been looking forward to it all week, so I answered for my pussy's sake.

"Yes Clay…I have plenty of it, black just so happens to be my favorite color."

"Look Lane let me get off the phone, just visualizing you I feel goodie coming to attention and I'm about to step into my first meeting. Give me a few and Shauna, my assistant, will call you and if you don't feel like driving I'll send a car for you."

"A car?"

"Yes a car. I don't want you to be out on the road driving unnecessarily, it sounds like you had a stressful two days with seeing your girl in her condition in the hospital. I just want to make things a little easier from you."

"That's sweet Clay, but I'll be alright."

"Okay. Just let me know if you change your mind, give me a buzz and I'll arrange it."

"I will."

"Alright Lane, see you tonight."

"Yes you will." From that one call, I'm so stimulated; I can't wait to get this day over. I vibrated just to think about what will take place tonight. Finally, after getting through the muck and mire of traffic, I got to work. My boss, with me and a few of my other colleagues, have a brief meeting. First order of business, Mr Wyatt applauds me for remaining so professional while dealing with Mr Akoyeiu. He confessed that Mr Akoyeiu called him and asked if he would bend the rules just so he could take me to dinner. I told Mr Wyatt how I tried to let him down easy because I was so afraid he would take his account elsewhere. Mr Wyatt assured me he knew I played by the rules, because he knew my character, in addition to Mr Akoyeiu informing him of such. He talked to the heads of each department concerning areas, which were of concern. He touched briefly on some new changes that would be taking place but, were still in the baby stages, so he would get back to us when it was time. Mr Wyatt concluded the meeting but asked me to lag back. The next thing he asked me was somewhat of a shock.

"Lane, you may think your work here goes unnoticed, but that's definitely not the case. You've been a consistent team player of this bank and I would like to know are your ready for another challenge?"

"Of course Mr Wyatt, and what challenge would that be?"

"You would be a corporate finance professional; you already hold a degree in accounting with emphasis in equity and mergers. You're knowledgeable of tax laws and implications and most importantly; your personality. You have a great sense of humor but with a no nonsense approach. Not to mention, how impressed I am that you can speak several different languages." I sat there flattered as hell. He had apparently done his homework on my background but before I let the flattery go to my head, I had to hear how this would benefit me as far as perquisites go. What should I be looking forward to; would I get to travel, a bigger office, and the million-dollar question, what kind of money was he talking about. All these questions popped into my head. I was not prepared to jump in with my eyes wide shut and say yes, no matter how wonderful it may have sounded.

"Mr Wyatt, I must say how pleased I am to know that you appreciate the work I'm doing here…but this sounds like a big deal. May I ask you to please allow me some time to think about it before I make a rush decision."

"Of course you can Lane, you're right; this is a big deal and I hope I didn't put you on the spot. Get back to me once you have considered it thoroughly. Furthermore what I'm about to tell you is confidential; so please don't let it leave my office."

"Of course Mr Wyatt, I will keep it in the strictest of confidence."

"Good... Theresa in Paying and Receiving has asked me about this position everyday since she heard that Rita was leaving, but I don't feel she'll be a suitable candidate for it. That's why I'm hoping that you will strongly consider my offer."

"Of course I will and thank you for your vote of confidence Mr Wyatt."

"No, thank you! Please just remember not to say anything about my offer I made you just yet."

"Most certainly... is this all for this morning; I have somewhat of an emergency that will take me away from the bank this morning, but I'll be back before lunch."

"Is there anything I can help you with?"

"No sir, my best friend is in ICU at Piedmont Hospital and I have been worried sick about her."

"Oh...Lane I'm sorry to hear that. You go and don't worry about returning before lunch; do you have anything pressing today? If so; just brief Rita, she can handle it for you so you take the rest of the day off and check on your friend." Wow, is this one of the perks that's being dangled in front of me, because if it is; I love it.

"Why, thank you so much Mr Wyatt I really appreciate this."

"Don't mention it, have a good weekend. I hope all will be well with your friend and think about what we talked about."

"I will and I'll stop by Rita's office before I go."

"Good, see you Monday Lane." I damn near skipped out of his office with the thought of having the rest of the day off. I wondered was this one of the top secret changes that was still in the baby stage he couldn't talk about. I will think hard about his proposal. Not only can I go see Faizon and check on the Hill's; I have plenty of time to prepare myself for Clay's homecoming. I kept my promise, stopped by Rita's office to inform her of the new account from Japan, and explained why I was leaving it in her hands. She too sent me off with well wishes for Faizon, and assured me all would be fine. I tried calling Char to let her know that I could meet her at the hospital after all, but her cell went straight to voice mail. I thought she might already be there; so I'll just meet her there. This should be the happiest time of my life, a new man and now a promotion, but I couldn't rejoice knowing that my best friend was clinging to life.I got to the hospital and no sign of Char, but the news I received when I got there made me forget all about her. I met the Hill's smiling faces walking towards the elevator, just the look on Mrs Hill's face let me know their princess was going to be alright.

"Lane..." Mrs Hill called gleefully, "I just called your job and they told me I just missed you. I had a feeling you were on your way up here. I tried calling Charmine as well, but I kept getting her voicemail."

"I tried calling her and got voicemail too, so I just left her a message. I know she had a meeting this morning. She may have gotten held up longer than expected anyway; you two are sure looking like a ray of sunshine. Mrs Hill; does Faizon have something to do with that?"

"Yes, she has everything to do with it. Lane, our baby is responding very well to the tests the doctors have run on her today. The doctors have said she'll be in her own room later today." Mr Hill looked ten years younger today, and was beaming with just as much joy as Mrs Hill. I heard it in his voice when he called out to his wife to tell me the best news.

"Patricia," Mr Hill calls out, "tell Lane the news!"

"Lane, he had me repeat this story all morning, and I'm tired of repeating it." Mrs Hill says playfully while rolling her eyes at Mr Hill.

"Ahhh now Pat, don't be jealous; go on and tell her." Just seeing the two of them being able to smile again made me laugh and beg Mrs Hill to tell me what had them so happy. "Roger is beaming because Faizon came to, asking for her daddy. Lane you know she has always been a daddy's girl, so I don't know why Roger is acting so shocked." She giggled while looking at her husband and he returned her smiles. "Yeah Lane, she woke up looking for me, and I was right there waiting on her. She asked me for some water and starbursts, like she used to do when she was a little girl." I was so glad to hear that. Usually my Friday's can be like my Monday's, but this had to be one of the best Fridays I've had in a long time and it wasn't over yet. I still had my Clay to look forward to.

"Mr Hill, will it be alright to see her today?"

"I don't see why not; she's being discharged from ICU into her own room. That's why Mrs Hill and I were downstairs getting some coffee. We haven't been able to eat or drink since this happened."

"Really, after she is walking out of here for good; I owe you and Mrs Hill a delicious meal."

"Lane, it might be a little while longer to get Princess set up in her room, so if you have anything you need to do; you might want to do it now."

"No, I'm here until I see Faizon today. I will try Char again; to let her know now will be a good time to come on."

"Good idea. Pardon me Lane; let me find out where my wife has disappeared to."

"Ok sir, I'll be in the waiting room. I walked into the waiting room to attempt to call Char's cell again, this time she answers and sounds a little flustered when she picks up.

"Hi. Hello this is Charmine."

"I know who you are, where are you?"

"Lane, where are you?"

"I'm at the hospital with Faizon and great news; she's alert and talking today. As a matter of fact she will be in her own room in a matter of minutes!"

"That's spectacular, and the Hills?"

"The two of them look like a ton of bricks have been lifted off of them, wait...where are you?"

"You'll never believe me."

"Try me."

"Anthony...I mean Mr Martin and I just slept together."

"You did what?"

"Why are you yelling, the Hills might hear you."

"No they can't, they're in the corridor, and I'm in the waiting room alone."

"I said Mr Martin..."

"Cut the Mr Martin shit out, you just fucked him. I think calling him Anthony is appropriate."

"Shut up Lane, you silly."

"Look, how far are you from the hospital?"

"I'm no where near able to get there. What I was supposed to be doing before I got to the hospital, I used that time being fucked by my boss. I cannot believe this shit. Did you just hear what I said...? I just slept with my boss."

"I heard you and we'll talk about that shit later. Right now

I'm going to see about Faizon. Call me when you're done with whatever you're supposed to be doing."

"Alright, kiss Faizon for me and tell the Hill's I'll be there today."

"Alright will do. I have to hear this from the beginning, but don't forget I'm out when Clay gets home; he's sending his car for me."

"A car...? Well you go Miss Holiday."

"Be quiet, I'll talk to you later." The conversation ended and just the thought of Char's situation with her boss caused me to be a little concerned. I pray she knows what she's doing and go to find the Hill's. I saw the Hill's standing by the room assigned to Faizon. It couldn't have been more than a few seconds that passed before I saw two hospital staff rolling Faizon to her new room on a stretcher. As she's closer, Mrs Hill and I meet her. Looking down at my friend I cringe with disbelief, at how her beautiful face has been disfigured by the abuse she took to her face and head area. I begged myself to keep it together and to just thank God, because it could have been a lot worst. Faizon opened her eyes and noticed me and her mom standing there waiting to greet her, she attemptted a weak smile but she just couldn't force one and turned away. Mrs Hill touched her arm and now Mr Hill has joined us. "Hello Princess." Mr Hill blared.

Faizon is still trying her best to smile and not shed a tear. The nurses approached her bed getting things set up to transfer her smoothly onto her new bed. They lift Faizon very carefully and in one motion; as a third nurse enters the room, prepares her IV, and starts checking her vitals. Faizon searched her new room until she finds the face of her dad and I could swear I heard her eyes scream out to him. The male nurse broke their silent communication by asking Faizon if she needed anything before he leaves the room. Faizon shakes her head no and looks around for her mother. Mrs Hill realizes this; she dashes to move in closer to Faizon and starts to cover Faizon's trembled body, while bending to plant loving kisses on her cheek. I've known Faizon for over a year and today I felt like a stranger as I timidly approached her. We exchange looks, I notice a tear escaping her beautiful eyes and I knew then things would never be the same for her. I took her hand and whispered to her not to worry.

Mr Hill suggested to his wife for them to get some coffee, while Faizon and I visited. Mrs Hill agreed and told Faizon they'd be back shortly. Faizon noded at her mother and watched her parents as they walked out of the room. I pulled a chair close to her bed and sat down. I took her cold hand and rubbed it between mine to warm it. I didn't know how to start the conversation, so I just opened my mouth.

"Faizon...I'm so sorry this happened to you; but we are so grateful that you're ...I couldn't even bring myself to finish my sentence. "We're so happy to see that you're alright."

"Where's Charmine?"

"Char had tons of work she needed to finish. She'll be here a little later, I just spoke to her just before you got into your room; she told me to tell you that she loves you and will see you later." She nods her head and takes her free hand and touches her forehead gingerly as she feels for her wounds. "Lane... every time I close my eyes I can still see him standing there, hitting me, repeatedly until I couldn't feel him anymore. I've never seem him like that." I could feel her reliving that moment as she squeezed my hand tighter as she reminisced her ordeal. I literally felt sick to my stomach to hear her talk about that morning. I couldn't help but think how alone she must have felt. Faizon started to cry aloud and continued to ask why, and how could he do something like this. I couldn't answer her, because I too wanted to know how could he do something like this to her. I touched her face gently and re-assured her it was nothing that she had done; apparently he was sick. "I told myself the first time he put his hands on me that I must have done something wrong. Did she just say the first time, so the motherfucker had done this before? I didn't want to pry but, I just had to know, not really sure if I was prepared to hear the answer. "Faizon....you just said the first time, so... he's done this before?" Faizon looked at me as she might as well come clean. The cat was already out the bag.

"Yes Lane this wasn't the first time; this was just the worst time."

"Why didn't you ever tell anyone what was going on?"

"How could I tell y'all what he was doing, I knew how everyone felt about him and knowing you, you would have told my dad and my dad would have killed him, and you know it."

"I do know that...but we could have figured something out. Why you felt the need to keep this dark secret to yourself; I don't know."

"Darnell was always making me feel so insecure and always told me how you and Charmine weren't my true friends, because I...,"

"Let me stop you Faizon, because I want to say this to you as gently as I can, because in the last two days you've been to hell and back. Please don't tell me nothing that bitch told you. I never, and especially now gave a fuck about Darnell. I smelled the motherfucker was a bad news from the moment I saw him. I'll end the conversation about him simply like this. I can't wait until the police catch him...he goes to jail... and he gets fucked with a sick dick. Then, and only then will I be extremely happy!" Why that seemed to bring a smile to Faizon's face, I don't know because I was dead serious, but I was so glad to see her smile. I would have said it again.

"Do you want me to do anything for you?"

"Umm...yeah, would you mind going to my house and grabbing my sketchbooks. My doctors are saying I may be here for awhile and I don't want to lose any ideas that may come to mind."

"Of course I will, I'll take care of that today. I'll just need your keys."

"No, you don't have to do it today I know you got to get back to work."

"Actually, I don't. My boss gave me the rest of the day off. I told him about you and he was so concerned, so he let me off."

"That was sweet of him."

"Yeah that was, so I'm free until tonight."

"What you doing tonight?"

"Clay comes back home tonight; he was in Philly on business." Faizon smiles and tells me I can get the keys from her mother. "Lane, I'm so blessed to have good parents and friends like you and Charmine in my life. I am so angry with myself allowing him to make me feel so inadequate and ugly." Faizon stares into the ceiling and starts to cry again. "Don't cry Faizon, we'll get through this together. He was projecting his own feelings of insecurities onto you; he just took advantage of your loving nature." After she heard that, she just cried harder.

"It's alright cry; you'll get better and stronger each day."

"What about mentally Lane...did my mother tell you anything else?" I looked at her, puzzled by her question thinking back if her mother has told me anything. Oh God, could she be speaking of the baby? I don't dare talk about it, just in case she wasn't talking about the baby. I don't know how much she knew, but because her dad told me; I could answer her honestly. "No, Faizon, was she suppose to tell me something?"

Faizon asked me to pass her a cup of water that was sitting on her tray. I helped her take a few sips from her straw before she continued. "No, she wasn't supposed to tell you because I asked her not to; I wanted to tell you and Char myself. Lane… I was pregnant with his child. I took a home pregnancy test twice on Wednesday just to be sure before calling him. I told him thinking he would be happy, but the next morning he arrived at my door with a look of rage on his face. I noticed he had a walking cane in his hand but I didn't think anything of it at the time. I was so shocked by his reaction. He was so cold and distant, he kept telling me over and over again he wanted nothing to do with the baby because…"and she takes a long pause and another sip of water before giving me the finale, "because he was married the whole time. When I told him that I was pregnant, he said that had nothing to do with him. When I told him I was still going to have the baby, he went ballistic. He hit me in my stomach first with the stick; I remember falling to the floor clutching my stomach trying my best to protect the baby and than he began hitting me in my head with the stick. I blacked out after feeling the third blow. The next thing I know, I'm in here."

I sat as still as a statue, listening to her torture. I was so angry and hurt for her at the same time, I couldn't help but cry. She gripped my hand even harder as her tears fell even faster. Moment's later the Hill's have returned to the room. I jumped up quickly and ducked into the bathroom. I didn't want the Hill's to know what we have been discussing. I knew they would die knowing the brutal details of what their daughter faced alone on that morning, and I prayed they never will. I sipped water from the bathroom sink in my cupped hands, splash some water on my face, and headed out to rejoin Faizon and her parents.

Mrs Hill looked at me and asks if everything is okay. I tell her I am fine and asked for Faizon's house keys. Mrs Hill digs in her purse and gives me her spare set. I walked over to Faizon, leaned over her bed and gave her a kiss. I hugged the Hills and told them I will be back later with Faizon's request. Mr Hill looked at me and offered to walk me to the elevator. He looked back at his family and told them he'll be right back.

As we walked, he stoped me by tugging my arm and asked me directly, what was Faizon and I talking about, that apparently disturbed me to tears. I tried to lie and say nothing but he wasn't buying it. I told him that Faizon was concerned about him retaliating against Darnell and getting into trouble. "I won't make no bones about it, I want that bastard and I want him to hurt like he hurt my daughter; but all in due time. The police have not caught up with him yet and for his sake he better pray that they do…before I do." He releases his grip on my arm and says he'll see me when I get back. I jumped on the elevator, I'm ice cold to my core just thinking about what I have just been told by Faizon. Until that moment, I've never considered myself to be a vindictive person, but I wanted Darnell to suffer like he caused Faizon to suffer before he disappeared.

Still feeling physically sick and wiped out, I'm so grateful that Mr Wyatt let me have the rest of the day off because after seeing Faizon in that condition, there was no way I could have returned to work. I had turned my cell phone off while in the hospital and turned it back on once I got in my car. It wasn't on a minute before my message alerts starts going wild. I started listening to my messages. The first message was from Clay making sure Faizon was all right, and that we were still on for tonight, one from my mother, a number I'm not familiar with and Charmine letting me know she would be at the hospital by noon.

I looked at my watch and it's a little after eleven, so I immediately called her back to see if she would meet me at Faizon's house.

I had to also admit to Char that I was feeling a little eerie about entering Faizon's house on my own after what took place there yesterday.

"What's up?"

"Where are you?"

"I'm just leaving the office heading your way, why?"

"Change of plans that's why, meet me at Faizon house."

"Why...what's going on."

"Nothing, Faizon wants her sketch pad so she can continue to draw once she's up to it."

"That's a good sign, how does she look?"

"There is no better way to put it, so prepare yourself. I felt sick looking at what that bitch did to her. Plus she knows she lost the baby."

"How do you know?"

"She told me, that's how."

"Wait Lane; take the bass out your voice. I know you're upset but I'm on your side. I'll tell you what; I'll just meet you at Faizon's."

"I'm sorry Char, you just shoulda heard all the shit she went through. You're gonna freak out on this part."

"What?"

"This wasn't the first time he abused her."

"What!?"

"You heard me right, this wasn't the first time; he abused her before."

"I can't believe what I'm hearing."

"You can't; I almost went through the roof, but what good would that do now?" After hearing this Char agreeed to meet me at her house. We hang up and I head in the direction of Faizon's house. I approached her house and sit in my car waiting for Charmine so we can enter the house together. It wasn't much later that she pulls up, gets out of her truck and starts to speed walk up the driveway. We're so stunned by all the events that have taken place, we just look at each other speechless; but our faces told the story. We embraced before I unlocked the door. "Does she look that bad?" Char asks. I had to be honest and tell her yes she did, but I was happy to report she was a trooper. I added she was alert and focused on her sketching and wanting to jump right back in the swing of things. "Char you know it will take a while for her to get back on her feet and that's why we're here, and the two of us; along with her parents will see her through this.

Chapter Seven

When we got inside we could see the havoc caused by that manic, lamps on the floor, family pictures smashed and then we see it, the blood...all that blood. I stood there frozen. I turned to look at Charmine, and she had the same lifeless look on her face. This was the final straw, my insides had to erupt, I ran to Faizon's bathroom and threw my guts up in her bathroom sink until I had nothing else in my system to come up. I felt so weak; it was as if I had taken a beating. I washed my face and gargled with some mouthwash before meeting Char back in the living room. Char stayed glued to that one spot as if her legs were cemented to the floor.

"Char...Char... are you alright?"

"Honestly I'm not; this was the act of an animal. Let's just get her things and be out." I could not have agreed more. I walked back to the room Faizon has made into her work area. I looked on her table where she normally sketches. I looked under fabric and doodles of her ideas that must have come to her in the spur of the moment, but no sketchpad. I continued to search all the areas I think it may be hiding. I walked over to her sewing machine and I spotted it in the wastebasket…each page of her new sketches, tattooed with her blood, with the word bitch over all of Faizon's beautiful designs, each and every page. That sick bitch, what possessed him? I knew then he was the devil. Why…what made him snap like this …why did he take it so far? I walked out of the room empty handed and with a look of bewilderment.

"Where's her stuff?"

"You aren't going to believe this shit; the motherfucker ruined all her designs."

"You're kidding me right?"

"Char, you know I'm not kidding about this, there's nothing about this shit that's funny."

"I don't understand. Why did he react this way? He was begging her to take him back this could have been a perfect way to get back in her good graces."

"There is a lot you don't know about."

"Like what?"

"Well for one, he was married."

"Married! Every time you open your mouth it just keeps getting worse and worse!"

"Yeah married, it's a long story and when Faizon is well enough or if she wants us to know the entire story she'll tell us. For right now we just have to help her keep her head on straight."

"Yeah you're right, let's boogey. What are you gonna tell her about her designs?"

"That's a good question, what am I going to tell her. I'll think about that on the way back."

126

"What time are you meeting Clay?"

"Tonight about nine, why?"

"After we leave the hospital, I want to talk to you about what happened with me and Anthony this morning."

"Oh yeah, please don't think because I haven't said anything, I forgot about that ridiculous ass shit."

"What's so ridiculous about it?"

"Are you being serious…? I don't have all night; plus we have to get back to the hospital. We'll have an opportunity to discuss it in detail at Sylvia's later this afternoon, my treat."

"Deal." I turned off the lights and we walked out of the house. Char walked ahead of me; I locked the door and turned to tell her I'll meet her at the hospital. We walked down the driveway and we both must have seen him at same time. We looked at each other in fucking disbelief. Darnell is sitting across the street peering at us through the gates of Faizon's subdivision in his tore back Honda watching us leave Faizon's house. When he sees us walk down the driveway, he starts his car and yells, "Ho's!," in our direction and speeds off. I couldn't get my cell out quick enough. Char dials 911 and starts shouting to the dispatcher that the man who nearly killed her friend just sped off in a teal Honda. I told Char to give the dispatcher his license plate, "The Don." We want the motherfucker caught before he gets too far. I called the Hills to let them know what has just taken place in front of Faizon's house. I informed Mrs Hill of the destruction we found when entering Faizon's home and made her aware that Char was on the phone with the police as we spoke. Mrs Hill yells, "Thank you Jesus", and that's when Mr Hill got on the phone to ask what is going on. I briefed him on Faizon's sketches, and Darnell's speedy get away.

He sounded disappointed that the police would have first crack at him, but happy to hear that we called the police. I told him that we would be back at the hospital shortly, and added I didn't know how to break the news to Faizon's about her designs. He told me to just be honest; she needed to know what kind of psychopath she was dealing with. I saw Charmine put her cell in her bag; I wanted to know what was said, so I ended the conversation with Mr Hill and asked Char what the police were saying.

"They're dispatching a car to look for him immediately, the dispatcher took my number and the Hill's number and will let us know when he is caught."

"Good, what an idiot...do you get him? Was he expecting to find Faizon here, does he realize he almost killed her?"

"I don't know and don't care what he thought; he can explain that shit to the police." We jumped in our vehicles and head to Piedmont hospital. I made it to the hospital before Char and decided I'll head on upstairs to tell Faizon why I couldn't bring her designs. I entered the room and the Mr Hill is on the phone talking to the police. Mrs Hill walks briskly over to me, grabs my hands, and informs me he's been caught before he even made it to interstate. "That's wonderful news." I looked over at Faizon, she doesn't look so thrilled, I looked at her mother and told her again how glad I am that they caught him before walking over to Faizon's bed. I pulled up a chair and sat down. Minutes later, Charmine finally makes it up to Faizon's room, and greets Mrs Hill. She asked if the police contacted them because they called her and she asked them to call Faizon's parent's who were already at the hospital.

Mrs Hill informed Charmine that's who her husband was on the phone with now. Charmine walked over to Faizon and me and kisses Faizon on her forehead. Faizon returns a weak smile and an equally weak hello.

"What's up Miss Georgia Peach, how ya feeling?"

"I could be better."

"Hell, we all could be better." I said trying to evoke laughter. Still beating around the bush on how to bring up her destroyed designs. I thought about what her dad said, and agreed to just get this over with.

"Faizon…"I start very apprehensively, "I didn't bring your sketches here with me, because…

"Why, you couldn't find them?"

"No I found them, it's just that…"

"He got to them didn't he?"

"Yes…he did. Faizon, I'm so sorry." Tears immediately dropped from her hazel eyes as she covered her face hoping not to let her dad see, but it was too late, he passed the phone to his wife and flew by her side. "Princess, don't cry, whatever he did you can re-do, he didn't win and you can't let him. He didn't expect you to survive, but you did. He thinks he can kill your dream, your spirit; by ruining a few sketches and he can't. Do you remember what I always told you as a teenager, only you, can break you, and that piece of shit can't break you. You are a Hill."

"I know daddy, it's just…,

"It's just nothing, when you get home, you'll start over. Simple as that." Mr Hill always had a firm way about him but it seemed to work. He wiped her tears on his handkerchief, offered her some water from her cup, adjusted her pillows and that was the end of that. When Mrs Hill got off the phone with the police she told Faizon that they were sending an officer to meet with her and take a statement. "It looks like he'll be charged with attempted murder and….murder of the unborn child. I was so happy to hear that I didn't know what to do.

Mrs Hill looked so tired; her once peaceful face, looked washed out. Her eyes had dark circles under them and her steps looked as through she was in pain with each stride. I suggested to Mrs Hill, that she should get some rest at home and we would make sure Faizon was not left alone until she comes back. At first, she looked at all of us, as she wasn't having any of it, until Mr Hill finally put his foot down. "Patricia, Lane is right, you're tired and you're gonna need all of your strength. I'm gonna need all of your strength. I can't think of both of my girls in the hospital. Please let me take you home so you can get some rest and we'll can come back together....please Patricia, this has been hard on all of us and I'm going to need you more now than you know." I could see Mr Hill had a loving control over his girls because when he spoke; they listened.

"Okay. Lane, I'll get some rest, but you and Charmine have to promise me that you'll stay with her until we return."

"Mrs Hill of course, we promise. We would never leave her in this condition."

"We promise." Char chimes in.

"I can't tell you two how nice it's been to have y'all here with us, helping to get us through this, Faizon couldn't ask for better friends. Thank you two so much." As she gave Charmine and me kisses, her tears moistened her dry face, while her husband walked over to her and placed her sweater over her shoulders. She walked over to her daughter and assured her she would be back before she knew it. Faizon looked at her exhausted mother and told her not to worry about coming back, that Charmine and I, would look after her and when we had to leave the nurses would be there. "Don't be silly Faizon, I just need to get some sleep, take a relaxing bath and me and your dad will be back." Faizon gave her a smile and a kiss and told her she would see her later since she insisted on coming back. Mr Hill caressed his daughter's face, placed a soft kiss on her cheek, and kissed her head bandage. He looked at us, thanked us again, and told us they wouldn't be long. We tried to encourage them to take as much time as they needed, and get the much needed rest that their bodies must have craved, but he wasn't hearing it. We stopped trying to convince them and told them we would see them when they got back. The Hills walked hand in hand out the room.

Char pulled the other chair close to Faizon's bed; she looked everywhere except at Faizon. For a while, we all just sat there not knowing what to do, or say. I looked around to see if there was a clock in the room, I spotted one near the patient's closet; ten minutes after two. I still had enough time to hear the story of the century between Charmine and her boss and get home before my date with Clay. A stocky nurse with the thickest glasses I've ever seen comes in and checks Faizon's vitals. After her routine check, the nurse announced that she is pleased to see that Faizon is doing well, especially considering she was discharged from ICU only hours earlier.

The nurse voiced her disgust on the situation, saying that she overheard the Hills discussing the matter amongst themselves. She announced she prayed for Faizon and hoped that the police would catch the "evil person", that could do such a thing. Charmine told her that her prayers was answered because the "evil person" was caught and is in jail. "Thank the Lord... thank the Lord. God is good." The concerned nurse says as she clasps her hands together in a praying position. Now, if you've ever been to church, whenever you hear someone say "God is good", you must say, "all the time." So we did. The nurse told us she would be back to check on Faizon within the hour, but not to hesitate to call her if we needed her before then, and showed us how to operate the call bell. We thanked her, and she left the room. I asked Faizon was she in pain, she said surprisingly she wasn't. She just hated that her parents had to suffer along with her because of what Darnell did. "I just wish I hadn't let him in. I keep re-playing it all in my head and I think about how I felt something just wasn't right with him. I've even heard Oprah say on her show a million times, "Listen to your instincts", and my instincts told me to not open my door and I did it anyway. I wanted to reason with him only to find out there was no reasoning, he just went berserk."

"Sshh sweetie, you couldn't have known he was going to go this far, what he did was despicable and cowardly. I knew there was something I never trusted about him." I just sat and listened while Charmine tries to soothe Faizon.

"I don't know how or what to feel about losing the baby, I think to myself; why do I feel numb when I think about it, shouldn't I be sad?" She questioned.

"Listen sweetheart, you've just been through a devastating ordeal. You're still in shock from what took place and you are probably still numb. Don't try to force an emotion, just allow your body to adjust at it's own pace."

"I agree Faizon, the body has a funny way of protecting itself, and shock is one of them. I hate to put it like this but once you get better, you'll have plenty of time to grieve." You can tell she was listening, but her eyes wandered to a far away place and I asked myself; would she ever be the same. I was glad when Charmine shifted the conversation to her and asked did we want to hear about her morning, because honestly…I was dying to hear about it. I sat on the edge of my chair as if I was watching a suspense movie.

"Hell yeah I want to hear about the boss and his slut."

"Watch your mouth, I ain't no slut." Faizon's attention was now back on us. I thought I'd better fill her in. "Yes, please get comfortable for this one Faizon, the feature film is about to start, starring Mr Martin as the Boss and Charmine Grant as the Slut." That seemed to amuse Faizon as she smiled a genuine smile for the first time all day.

"If you're gonna be an ass, I'll keep it to myself."

"Aahhh... stop being a baby. You knew I was gonna fuck with you, because I told you this shit was gonna happen. It was you who kept saying, Noo, he's my boss, nothing is going on, and our relationship is purely professional. Professional my ass, I was just waiting for you two to slip up."

"Do you want to hear what happened or not!"

"Shit, if she doesn't I sure do." Faizon answers and attempted to scoot her body closer to the rails of the bed to get a better view and in listening range of Charmine.

"Okay...it's so crazy I can't believe it myself. We had a scheduled meeting at the downtown Marriott with a few other partners of the firm and some out of town clients. Anthony and I decided to meet a little earlier so he could brief me on the new clients and tell me how he wanted me to handle them. So there I was having my usual cup of morning tea and he ordered a coffee."

"Please spare us the drink orders, and tell us the good shit!"

"I'm trying if you'll stop interrupting me; well anyway we are having our drinks when he comments on how nice I looked today. I had just taken a bite of a warm buttered croissant and was about to say thank you, when some melted butter dropped on my lip. He wipes the butter off with his fingers and seductively sucks the butter off. Stunned, I just stared at him not knowing how to respond until he say's I had some more on my lip, but this time he takes his finger with the butter on it and puts it in my mouth. Instinctively I began to suck his finger, making sure all the butter is off. I knew then we were at the point of no return. He then leans in and gives me this erotic kiss, and I didn't pull back. I just let it happen, so there we were; sitting at the table of the Marriott kissing like we were on a date and not a business meeting that was about to take place in a little over an hour. Then Anthony glances at his watch and makes a beeline out of the meeting room. When he returns, he grabs my hands and leads me to the elevators. The next thing I know, we're in room 1123 making love."

"What do you mean, the next thing you know, did he drug your tea?"

"No!"

"So you were fully aware and consented to the fucking of your boss."

"Of course it was consensual, Lane." Faizon has now totally perked up, as if she was watching a daytime story and asks, "How was it?"

"I can't lie," Charmine starts to sing, "He can't work the middle cuz his thing's too little." All three of us cracked up off that.

"But I'll tell you what; he can eat the hell out some pussy. He had me pulling the sheets and the pillowcases off the bed."

"Whhaaat, that must have been some good eating."

"Shut up, that's why I hate telling you shit."

"Stop lying girl, you know I make your day with my bullshit, but for real, his shit was that small because knowing how to eat pussy is important, but that can't replace a hard dick." Faizon just shakes her head, but agrees with me.

"Charmine, you know Lane is telling the truth, it's just something about a stiff one."

"Aahh the dead has arisen to comment on the topic of dick. I'm sure your parents will be glad to hear this when they return."

"You wouldn't dare tell them what we're talking about."

"Of course not! I don't want your parents to think I'm a bad influence." Charmine chuckles, but gets a serious look on her face and asks; what is she going do now?

"What did he say after he got through waxing that pussy?"

"Nothing really, just that he wanted to do that from the day I walked into the interview with the firm and it was long overdue."

"Okay, what I should have asked, does he want to see you again?"

"He'll see me everyday. I work with him."

"Duuuh, I know that. You know what I'm talking about. Did he say he wanted to see you again romantically?"

"Yes he did, and that's where the problem is...I don't know if I want to see him like that again."

"Say you're joking, because guess what...it's literally too fucking late. Good or bad, you made a choice and because of that choice, you could possibly lose your career. A career you've worked so hard for. You better think about what you're saying, because losing a six figure salary just because someone can eat some pussy doesn't match."

"Look Lane, I know you are trying to help, but I don't need you to remind me of what's at risk. I am not saying that I don't want to see him again romantically. I just want to be sure. I can't jump from relationship to relationship."

"What's that suppose to mean, are you trying to insinuate that's what I do."

"Well you know the saying, if the shoes fit...."

"Fuck a shoe, I'm asking you, is that what you're saying."

"Whoa ladies, this is getting out of hand. Don't forget where you two are at and that y'all are suppose to be babysitting me or should I call my parents back here early because you two are acting like children." When Faizon asked us that, it brought me back down. This was not the appropriate time to have this kind of discussion. "I'm sorry Faizon we both should be ashamed of ourselves."

"Me too..." Charmine tells her," you should be used to the way Lane and I speak to each other, so get over it." Irritated, we turn our attention to the TV and start to watch some of Jerry Springer and his ridiculous re-runs. Faizon wonders out loud how he could still be on after all these years. I had to inform her because nosey people like us, kept him on.

The phone rings and Charmine picks it up, she talks a few minutes before hanging up. When she gets off the phone, she informs Faizon that, that was her dad and they're on their way back up to the hospital. Faizon asked why so soon, and Charmine told her the police had contacted her parents and said they were on their way, and her parents wanted to be present when they took her statement. Faizon gets that far away look in her eyes again and turns her face back towards the window. I asked Charmine did she want a soda from the vending machine and Faizon did she want me to ask her nurse if she could have anything else besides water or juice. They both turned my offer down, so I decided that I could wait as well.

It wasn't much later that the Hills returned looking a little more rejuvenated and was glad to see Faizon was still alert. Mr Hill walked over to her and kissed her in the same places as he did before he left and asked her did Charmine and me treat her all right. She looks over at us and asks us do we think we treated her well in her parent's absence. We both gave a nervous laugh and Faizon gets us both off the hook by telling her dad they left her safe with us. "Good sweet pea, I'm glad to hear that." Mrs Hill says as she joins her husband and daughter and gives us her look of approval. Mr Hill doesn't beat around the bush and asks Faizon was she ready to make a statement against Darnell? There's that look again, her dad asks her was she in pain and she answers no, but tells him she was thinking about what she should say.

"Tell them what happen. What do you mean what should you say!"

"Daddy…I just want this to be over and I 'm not sure if it will be, if I make a statement. What if he gets bailed out, he'll come for me."

"There's no way in hell that will happen. I'm here and even if you don't give a statement, what he did was a crime. The statement is just to give the police the accounts of what happened and they will take it from there. Charmine and I look at each other realizing that this is our cue to leave, this was a private family matter, and they needed to be alone.

"Boy, look at the time, we better be going."

"Lane is right, we better shove off."

"Don't let us push you out; y'all know ya'll can stay."

"Thanks Mr Hill, we know…I can't speak for Charmine but I have plans tonight, so I should really be heading out."

"I understand. I want to thank the both of you for watching my …our baby. Me or my wife will call y'all after the police have come and gone."

"Thank you Mr Hill, that would mean everything to me and I 'm sure I can speak for Lane." I nodded in agreement and reminded the Hills to call us if they needed us for anything. Charmine and I kissed Faizon and her parents and walked to the elevator. When we reached the elevator, I pressed the down button and we waited in total silence for it to arrive. When the elevator doors opened, we walked in and I hit the button for the lobby. It was not until we exited the hospital, Charmine said something to break the icy silence. "That poor thing, she must be going through hell. I can't imagine what she must be feeling." I didn't respond right away, still salty from the comment she made earlier.

"Lane, did you hear me?"

"Oh yeah…my mind was somewhere else." I lied, "Yeah it must be hell for her. What time do you have?"

"Its 4:45."

"Oh shit, I need to get to the house. Clay's expecting me at nine."

"I thought you was treating me to Sylvia's, you changed your mind?"

"I was only treating you to Sylvia's, so you could tell me about your fuckfest, but you already told us upstairs."

"Well ain't that nothing, if I knew that I would have kept your ass in suspense."

"Nah, but look at the smile you brought to Faizon's face. It was worth it don't you think."

"Yeah…it was worth it." We both approached our vehicles. I'm prepared to jump in before Charmine stops me one last time.

"What are you doing tomorrow?"

"I can't say right now, other than I know I'll visit Faizon for sure."

"Alright, call me so we can hook up, and get over it." I knew exactly what she was talking about and just said, I had gotten over it. Before heading to my car, I also told Char about my news of my promotion, and my apprehension to accept the offer. Char reminded me that was the reason I went to college to have offers like this basically given to me, but somehow it just didn't feel the same. She even tried to pick my spirits up by offering to take me out to celebrate, but I asked her if we could wait until Faizon got out of the hospital. She said she understood fully.

140

Chapter Eight

We hopped in our cars and headed in different directions. As soon as I got in, I called my parents to make sure that my home front was doing fine and thanked God, that it was. My mother told me that she and my dad was headed out to Junior's for dessert. I told her to eat enough for the both of us; she just laughed and promised she would. I found a comfortable, but sexy outfit for me to put on after a hot shower. When I got out, I called Clay and asked him did the offer still stand for his car to pick me up and he said it was on its way. Before I hung up he told me he couldn't wait to hold me. I got dressed quickly and because my hair was not co-operating, I had to wear it in a ponytail.

I packed a small cosmetic bag, and placed a new, one-piece teddy in it; I hoped Clay would love. I packed a few more essentials in my Louey V, and drank a glass of wine to settle my nerves from the emotionally draining day. I looked at my watch, and realized the time was now 8:05, I quickly finished off my wine. When my phone rings, it's Clay's driver telling me he will be here in less than two minutes. I thanked him and gathered my things. By the time I got outside; he has kept his promise and is standing by the passenger's back door to let me in.

"Good evening Ms. King, it's nice to meet you."

"Thank you and same here." I returned his banter. I sat in the back seat of the all black Towne car and closed my eyes, taking in the day and just thinking about how the night was going to end. I was getting antsy just thinking about Clay's touch, and how I needed to be in his arms tonight...definitely tonight. The driver took us to a beautiful sub-division in Atlanta. Some of the houses were huge, almost mansion- like. I thought to myself how nice it would be to own one of these homes one day, maybe sooner than later; with the promotion Mr Wyatt had talked to me about earlier today. The driver pulled in the driveway of this gorgeous two-story brick home with the lawn so manicured it looked unreal. Damn, he's living like this? I could only imagine what the inside looked like. The spiraled driveway alone looked like something out of a movie. The driver parked the car, jumped out, and opened my door. He got my bag and told me to enjoy my evening. I thanked him for the safe ride and getting my bag. Before I could even ring the bell, Clay jerked the door open and pulled me in; he began kissing me all over my face and neck. I returned his kisses like I was starving and inhaled all of him. From his loc's to his body, he smelled delicious. He stopped kissing me long enough to get my bag and gave me a much needed hug.

"Damn I missed you! I'm so glad you made it tonight."

"I missed you too Clay, you have a beautiful home."

"I'll give you a tour in a moment; just let me look at you again." I started to feel a little self conscious as he twirled me around and looked at me from head to toe and just grinned.

"What is in your bags....I hope overnight things?"

"No..., but it is something special for you." I replied with seductive eyes and lips, hoping he would get the picture. He must have because he didn't ask me anything else.

"Where do you want me to start the tour, upstairs or down?"

"Where ever you want to start."

"You sure?"

"Yeah, really."

"In that case I'll start downstairs because when we get upstairs; I think we might be there for awhile." I was saying in my head fine with me. I've been looking forward to this all week. Clay shows me his studio/office that he designed himself. Next was the living room, it showed his great taste in art and furniture. The artwork was remarkable; he had several priceless pieces that he picked up as he visited different countries. We made it as far as the kitchen, when he stands behind me so close, I can feel his dick growing against my ass. I turned my body to face him. I moved his loc's from his strong jaw and circled my tongue in his ear and neck, while slipping my hands down the back of his pants pulling him closer to me. I felt him continue to grow with each brush of my tongue on his neck. He lifts me and sits me on his beautiful marbled Island. He pulls my blouse opened and cups my breasts with both his hands and placed them in his mouth. Frenzied, I pulled him yet closer by wrapping my legs around his waist. I'm in a daze, so I faintly hear my cell phone going off, but I'm in no hurry to answer it until it continues to ring. I didn't want to answer it but with my mother not feeling her best, and Faizon barely out of ICU, I thought I'd better get it. Reluctantly, Clay helps me off his counter. Disgusted, I went to answer my cell. I looked to see who could it be and there was that unfamiliar New York number again.

"Hello…", and all I hear is,

"This is Rikers Island. You have a collect call from…Andre Floyd. Do you accept the charges?" Shit, it's Dre! What the fuck do I do? If I say no, he could need me. If I say yes, what will Clay think? I pondered my decision for a second longer and concluded I had to accept, Clay will understand. I tried to talk as low as I can. "Yes, I will accept." Dre is now talking to me, and I don't know what to say.

"Lane…baby… it that you?"

"Yes, Dre, it's me. What…why…why are you calling me…how did you get my number?"

"I got your number from your cousin Beverly. She was up here on a visit, and I asked her your number. Lane I've been dying to talk to you. I've been locked up for a minute. They're trying to say I murdered some dude I ain't never even heard of, or seen before."

"I know, my mother told me about it a few weeks ago."

"So you knew; why haven't you tried to contact me."

"Dre… are you serious? What do you mean why haven't I tried to contact you. That's not my job anymore remember… that's Renee's job."

"So what are you saying, you don't love me anymore?" I hesitated when he asked me that question because if he wanted a truthful answer, it would have been yes, but I had to cover up my feelings. I was about to answer him, when I felt Clay's presence in the room, I looked at him, and whispered I would only be a minute more. The look on his face made me realize I had less than a minute. I was hoping he would walk off, but he didn't budge from that spot.

"Dre… you caught me at a bad time. I can't talk right now."

"What do you mean you can't talk? Are you with

some nigga?"

"No, I just can't talk now. Call me tomorrow."

"No Lane, I need to talk to you now!"

"Dre…, tomorrow." I hung up before he kept me on the phone any longer. I looked around to apologize to Clay, but he just walked off and sits on his couch. I walked over and sat in a leather chair opposite him. I just looked at him and thought about what to say before I decided to speak, but he beats me to the punch.

"Lane, is there anything I need to know?"

"No…I just need to apologize for that call. That was an old friend of mine who's in trouble and needed to talk to me."

"I got time."

"For what?"

"The truth…just be honest. I'll respect that and you a whole lot more." Why didn't I just come clean, I'm not helping my reputation with him by continuing with these lies.

"All right Clay, that was my ex Dre. He's in trouble, he was arrested for murder a few weeks ago. He said he got my number from my cousin and this is my first time hearing his voice since he's been arrested." Clay continues to sit and look as though, he is trying to figure out if I'm telling the truth or not.

"So why didn't you just say that the first time, do you still have any feelings for him?"

"No…No. Its been over between us." There I go with the lies again, but how could I tell the man, I want to build a relationship with, I'm still in love with the man who broke my heart and is the reason I'm living in a whole new state. "Listen, I don't want this to interfere with our night but I need to be honest with you. I'm feeling you…I've already told you that, but like I told you from the gate. I'm a busy man and I don't have time for games. Do you remember on our first date, you asked me about my last relationship and I told you I ended it?"

"Yeah, I do remember."

"It ended because all she wanted to do was play games, one after another. Lies… jealously…just bullshit all the time… time that I didn't have to waste. And I am proud of what I've accomplished; not just my business, but how I handle my business, personally and professionally. I gotta tell you this Lane, from the start I felt that you and I have the chance to make this happen, but it's gotta be minus the bullshit, because it can end before it even starts. I don't want this to sound like threats, but I need for you to hear and understand what I am saying."

What he said hit me like a Mack truck, but I had to respect everything I heard him say. He could not have made it any clearer. I just hoped I could give him what he wants and deserves. All that he asked for is just plain honestly, but I cannot tell him I just lied to him about my feelings for Dre. I don't want this to be over before it starts. I leave my chair to join him on the sofa, to try to pick up where we left off in the kitchen, but he wasn't impressed. He got up and walked to the bar he had in his living room and poured himself a drink. As he poured his drink, I couldn't help but think how fine he is and how I wanted so badly to be with him. He walks over to me and offers me a sip of Hennessey from his glass. I accept while he's still holding the glass. "Clay I'm sorry. Let me make it up to you." I pull my black requested teddy out of my bag and hold it in front of me. Instead of him taking me by my hand and leading me upstairs as I hoped, he hits me with some shit from left field. "Let's grab something to eat and then I'll take you home." Shit, I'm being dismissed. I don't know who to be angrier at, Dre for calling, Beverly for giving him my number or me for answering the phone.

"Clay I apologized. I want to stay with you tonight; I've been waiting to be with you all week."

"I know that's what you think, but I want you to be sure. I'm not willing to compete with ex lovers, I don't have to. So when you know who and what you wanna do... I'm here." He grabbed my bag and waited for me to walk to the door. I'm walking but I can't believe what has taken place. I was about to plead my case one last time, but he opened the door before I could open my mouth. I realized he wasn't willing to listen, so with that, I conceded and we walked to his car.

For the first time I climbed in without him opening my door. I knew this thing with Dre troubled him. He got in and asked me where I wanted to eat. "Nowhere Clay, please just take me home." He obliged without further conversation. I sat there confounded with every fiber of my being, I wanted to plead to him not to take me home, but I had my pride. He drove the entire way in silence until we pulled up in my driveway. He looked at me like he's even having second thoughts, but instead of giving in; he leaned in, kissed me on the lips and sucked on my bottom lip before he pulled away. When I opened the door, he stayed seated. I knew he was upset because he did not attempt to escort me from his car.

"Lane... I want you; but I want you without your past relationships."

"I know you may not believe me but I want you too, please call me tomorrow Clay."

"Naahh.. I'm not gonna call you, you can call me; but when you're free of Dre."

"I'm free of Dre now, how can I convince you?"

"You don't have to convince me, convince yourself. Then give me a call me, Goodbye Lane."

Relay-tionships

150

Chapter Nine

I wasn't even get inside my house before I heard his car speed off. No, not again. I can't continue the path I've been taking with men. I'm in my thirties, educated, attractive and I have a lot to offer any relationship, so why the drama still. I stopped by my cabinet and fixed myself a Baileys before heading to my bedroom to throw myself on the bed. I tried calling Charmine, but her phone went straight to voicemail. No doubt, she is with Anthony and good for her, no need for both of us to be miserable. I jumped up and found some music to keep me company. It was apparent that I was in for the night.

I popped in my Kelly Price CD, "Soul of a Woman", laid on my bed and reminisced on the early days of me and Dre, and asked myself was it me that sent him looking elsewhere. I thought I was giving him everything he needed. I wanted to give him more than I gave Greg, but maybe 1 couldn't, because I wasn't fully over Greg. All I know is that I want Clay and Clay won't have me until as he say's, I'm free of Dre, and how do I do that. I still missed Dre; it wasn't like I was ready to end the relationship; I was forced to when I found him in Renee's pussy in our home.

As Kelly Price serenaded me in the background. I found myself tasting my own salted tears that streamed down my face involuntarily. What a day, between Faizon, Charmine, Dre, and now Clay; fuck it I had to get drunk. I hopped up, hurried into my bathroom to wash my face and pranced back up front to my living room where I poured myself a proper drink. I thought, as of tonight my love life was over, so I will consider the job offer that Mr Wyatt proposed to me earlier today.

If I can't have the man I want, at least I'll make the money I want. I danced by myself in my living room, masking the pain I felt, not knowing how to really deal with what I was going through. I didn't want to face the facts of my feelings for Dre, but I knew I had to deal with it. Tonight proved too much for me, I could possibly end up without Clay and I wasn't prepared for that. What I've learned of Clay so far, I deserved a man like him. I'm worth someone who will appreciate me, and he does deserve me, but without the excess baggage I'm carrying. It is up to me to work this Dre thing out, but how; especially now that he is locked up. The next time he calls, I must release my feelings so I can move on.

I must not have realized how tired I was, because a few more songs and a few more drinks, I was sprawled out on my couch until the next morning. I woke up to a splitting headache and an empty stomach. Once I collected myself, I prepared to take a quick shower and find something to do to keep myself busy today. While I showered, I decided to treat myself to getting my nails and hair done after I visit Faizon. Now dressed, I fried myself a quick egg sandwich; with my mouth watering, I'm prepared to sit and eat when the phone rings, please let it be Clay.

"What's up girlie?"

"Nothing Char, I'm about to eat this egg sandwich I fixed before I head out."

"Okay…. what's your plans for today?"

"I'm going to see Faizon of course, and after that get my hair and nails done."

"Mind if I tag along?"

"When have I ever minded that, actually I would love the company today."

"Why, what's going? Wasn't last night your big night out with Clay?"

"I didn't have a night with Clay."

"Why…?"

"We'll talk about that when I see you."

"What time do you wanna hook up?"

"What time is it now?"

"It's nearly noon."

"Shit, I had no idea it was that late, uumm… lets plan to meet at the hospital by one, I gotta eat something."

"That's what's up. I'll see you at the hospital."

"Alright, see you later sweetie." We hung up and I continued to devour my egg sandwich. When I arrived at the hospital, before I head upstairs I checked and re-checked my phone to make sure I haven't missed any calls. I was hoping Clay would reconsider and call me anyway, thus far he kept his word and he hadn't called. I reached Faizon's room and was met by her parents, Charmine, and one of her college friends whom I've heard her speak of but never met. I greeted the Hills with a kiss, and tapped Charmine on her arm. I introduced myself to Faizon's friend and before telling me her name, she looked me up and down as if I had done something wrong. "Hey... I'm Camilla," and she gives me this, did-you-wash-your-hands-kind of hand shake. I wanted to tell her "hay" was for horses but I knew that was childish, so I just relished in knowing that Charmine and I was going to jones the shit out of her, in private. The entire time she visited with Faizon, she dusted the chairs each time she sat down, she talked down to us, and appeared disgusted when she discovered that Charmine and I worked for a living. I was so glad when I heard the bitch say she had to leave, I damn near applauded.

I could tell that the Hills were just as pleased of her exit, because Mrs Hill, who always has a warm disposition, didn't even thank her for visiting. When she finally left, I asked Faizon, what was her girl's problem. Faizon explained that she was one of her sorority sisters who married into wealth and never worked a day in her life. Charmine said she was about to lay into her, when she talked so badly against attorneys but decided against it, realizing that she wasn't worth her energy.

Faizon was looking much better today, some of her color had returned to her lovely face and her eyes had that hazel sparkle back. Charmine asked her what the doctors were saying about her being released. Mr Hill answered for her saying that although she was looking better; due to the head trauma she suffered they wanted to keep her at least another week to make certain she suffered no brain damage. I wanted to ask how did the police report go but I didn't want to disrupt the mood. Faizon appeared to be in a much better space and even joined in when Charmine and I made fun of her whack ass friend Camilla. Charmine and I visited with Faizon another hour or so, before proceeding with the second leg of our day.

"Where would you like to get your nails done?" Charmine asks.

"There's a shop in Stone Mountain I like."

"Why way out there?"

"Well for one, I like it and second my hair salon is in Stone Mountain, so I might as well."

"You can still get your hair done in Stone Mountain, but there's this place in Buckhead that's really nice and isn't so crowded on Saturday mornings. Once she said that I was sold, because I knew the nail shop I was referring to, would be crammed. We decided to drive my car and come back for Charmine's truck. She complained of how the gas was killing her pocketbook, on her truck. Once we got in the car, I asked her about her night with Anthony, she gave me this stunned look before she answered.

"How did you know I was with Anthony last night?"

"I tried calling you when I got home from my blotched date with Clay."

"Oh yeah, what happened with the date of the century?"

"You first."

"It was a night I will long remember, and forget about what I said to you and Faizon in the hospital, he does know how to work the middle." She starts to giggle as if that was her first time making love.

"So dude grew insta-inches in less than twelve hours?"

"No...!"

"So does ole boy have a big dick or not?"

"No, and that's not important...well. It's just that yesterday morning we both may have been too nervous and he came to quick, but last night… we were more at ease with each other and he took his time. I really enjoyed being with him."

"Well, I'm glad one of us got fucked."

"Will you tell me what happened."

"Dre, that's what happened."

"What does Dre have to do with you and your night with Clay?"

"Clay was about to take me upstairs to tour the rest of his house and my body, when Dre calls collect on my cell."

"Don't say you accepted the charges, knowing you were on a date."

"Yeah, I'm still beating myself up for that one, but it gets better. He goes on to tell me how he needs me, wants me and how he is still in love with me and I better not be with another nigga."

"Please say you're joking, and you continued to listen to that nonsense while at another man's house. Lane, come on, wake up! You must know he is pulling your leg again. Why didn't you ask him why he didn't call Renee?"

"I asked him that, he said he didn't want her anymore."

"Lane be serious. A nigga in jail wants to be with anybody who wants to be with them. What he meant to say was she didn't want to be with him. You know that hook is about her money; now that he's in jail she is gonna hook with someone else. Be smart Lane, I don't know why you can't let go of him; do you remember how you found him in your bed?"

"Yes, I do remember and even after all that, I don't know why I can't let him go, but if I want to be with Clay, I've got to let go. Once Clay found out that I was talking to Dre, he cut our date slam off, and told me to contact him only when I am completely free of Dre."

"Well… I don't blame him Lane. Speaking from experience, you can't enter a new relationship with previous lovers still in the mix and expect it to be all good. Look what happened with Kamel and me. He always compared me to her, if not with his words with his eyes. He never was truly rid of her, and I kept begging him to be true to himself, so in turn, he could be true to me. He kept denying his true feelings for her until our wedding day and there I was …alone," Charmine's face took on a look of melancholy, I haven't seen her display in a while when talking about men, "and you know the rest of the story."

"I know and I have always admired how you bounced back from that, I don't know if I could have done it."

"Yes you could have, God gives us all the strength. You just have to find it, like now Lane…Dre is no good for you. I'm not saying he never loved you, because I believe at one time he did, but somewhere the love and respect disappeared, and that's what caused him to think he could bring women in your relationship, and in your bed."

"Believe me I hear everything you are saying to me and I'm going to put a stop to this one sided love affair I'm having with Dre."

"When Lane?"

"The next time he calls. I will dead it for real; I have to."

"Time will tell…time will tell." We pulled up at the nail salon and it was as empty as Char said and we had time for a manicure and pedicure. We hadn't been out of our chairs for longer than two minutes before Char gets a call from Anthony wanting to see her for lunch, so she bailed on getting her hair done. I dropped her back off to get her truck and I made my way to Stone Mountain to Hair We Are.

As I'm driving I rehearsed what I'm going to tell Dre the

next time he calls. I just need to let him know how I feel, and how badly he hurt me, when I found him and Renee in our home. I never had a true opportunity to let him know that because I wanted to get as far away from him, and that bitch as quickly as I could. By the time, I moved to Atlanta, I involved myself in work so deeply, I didn't have time to focus or deal with my true feelings about the matter, but now I had to face them or I could not move forward. I realized that last night.

I really wanted Clay last night and not just for sex because I could have gotten that from anywhere, but I really wanted him. I know I just met him, but I admire his swagger. I pulled into Hair We Are and see a hundred heads that are screaming out for help. I walked over to Niecy to let her know I've finally made it and she already had someone in her chair. "You're late, so you're next" She chastises me with a grin. "I know, the traffic was horrible this morning." Niecy summoned her shampoo girl to wash my hair, while she finished up with her other client. After my hair is washed, I grabbed a hair book, a seat, and waited to be next in Niecy's chair. I sat longer than I would like to sit in any salon, but I've been coming to Niecy since I moved to Atlanta, and she is definitely worth the wait. I saw Niecy spin her client around to her mirror and the woman gave her the universal nod of approval. Niecy sprayed her hair as the final touch. Niecy beckoned for me to take the chair as she and the woman handled the payment part. After they bid their farewells, Niecy came over and shields my clothes with a black protector.

"Hello Lane, good to see you."

"Good to see you too."

"What are you having done today?"

"Uuumm, just do what you do. I do know I need my ends clipped."

"Yeah I see." Niecy's chuckled as she ran her fingers through my hair, as if her thoughts were, I needed to be ashamed of myself. In an hour and miracle later, I'm ready for the world. Looking in the mirror, confirmed why I came to Niecy, because she's the best. I paid her and walked out of her salon, feeling like a million bucks. The feeling was quickly replaced with the thoughts of who am I looking like a million bucks for. Clay hasn't called me and I don't think he will. I jumped in my car knowing I still had most of the day ahead of me, what am I going to do? Clay had gotten me in the mood to fuck and since that didn't happen, I still feel the need to be loved, so I must take care of this feeling. Although I don't have a lot of fuck buddies, I have enough to help me out for today.

I made the decision that when I get home, I need to make a couple of phone calls to get my needs met. I reached home and called my mom first. I almost felt dirty while I talked to her; knowing what my intentions were after I hung up. If my mother only knew what I was up to, she would be flipping my pictures over, so thank God she still thought of me as her good little girl. I was glad to hear that she was doing better. I didn't tell her about the conversation I had with her doctor, I didn't want her to think I didn't trust what she reports from her doctor. He told me she was all right but wasn't following his instructions on keeping her diet and exercise regime. I did tell her no more catfish at night, she laughed but agreed. I told my mother that I will talk with her and dad tomorrow and hung up.

Now, I can take care of myself. I scrolled down my phone to see who the victim will be. I quickly passed Bernard's number, he's the type of brotha that thought his shit was all that and as soon as his dick was in you, he busts a nut and I needed more than a minute man today. Colin, Hell no! He always smells like he just got through eating onions. I get to Harris, Oh yeah, he's a prospect. He's good to look at and he smells good, plus he is attentive to every inch of my body, yes Harris it is and I connected the call.

"Hello Harris, this is Lane. How have you been?"

"What's good Lane, I haven't heard from you in a minute."

"Yeah I know, I've been so busy with work and other personal matters, I just lost touch, but that's why I'm calling you today. I've been thinking about you a lot lately and I was hoping that I could see you today." Yes, I know I lied but sometimes you must do and say shit you don't mean to get what you want, and besides; he won't know the difference.

"Hell yeah, I'll get up with you. I'm with my boys right now handling some business, but I won't be too much longer, you still at the same address?"

"Yes, call me if you change your mind Harris, see you soon."

"I ain't going to change my mind, I'll see you later alright? Bye Lane." I can't believe I just made a booty call but men do it all the time, so I grabbed something to drink and freshened up. I pulled out my red matching bra set to match the devilish mood I was in. I selected the music to put in the CD player to keep the flow right. An hour nearly passes when I hear my doorbell ring. I jumped up and got the door.

"What's up.?"

"Hi Harris, come in." He looked bigger than what I last remembered, but he was still nice to look at. He comes in; throws his body on my sofa and tells me he likes what I did with the house, referring to the new furniture and the wine cabinet I had put in.

"Thanks Harris, how have you been?"

"I'm good, working hard to stay on top."

"That's good to hear. I bet you were shocked to hear from me today."

"Nah, not really. I know the last time I was with you; I hit you off sumthin lovely. So I knew it was only a matter of time before you would want some more." Okay… I know the fuck he didn't just say that shit out loud, but because I need to be held, I'm going to have to act as though I didn't hear that. I gave him a phony ass laugh and asked him would he like something to drink. "Yeah, gimme a rum and coke if you have it." Harris requested.

"Sure I do, would you like ice?"

"Yeah, thanks." I head over to the bar to fix us a drink. After giving Harris his drink, I sat beside him on the sofa. I took a few sips of my drink while bobbing my head to the music I selected. Harris knew what my call was about and didn't waste any time. He sat his rum and coke on the table and started to rub my back. I can't lie his hands are feeling so nice. Harris used his free hand to massage his own dick. I was just about to get him right, until he had to open his mouth. "Lane, come here and get this medication you're addicted too." While he fumbled to pull his shit out of his pants. Morti-fuckinfied, I know this stupid ass doesn't think I'm about to suck his dick! I made the call, he does not get to call the shots, I protest! He has just fucked up the mood. I hopped off my couch like I was pricked by a diseased needle and looked at him and his dick." Harris I've made a terrible mistake ."

"What's the problem?"

"Calling your ass, you just don't pull your shit out and expect me to drop to my knees!"

"So why did you call me?"

"Not for that shit, so you can just put your shit back into

your pants and leave!" I was so heated I was almost stuttering.

"You lonely ass chicks bug me out! I decided I wouldn't respond to that, because what would my comeback be, "Yeah I know I'm lonely, so what." So I waited while he took his time putting his shit neatly back in his pants and finishing his drink. He was so pissed he didn't even close my door behind him. I walked over, slammed my door and thought I was glad that was over. I never considered myself desperate but that was a desperate move. I thought how all of this could be resolved if I had Clay with me for now and always. I threw my dirty dishes in the sink to wash later on and returned to my bedroom to work on my laptop. I'm having trouble concentrating, so I decided to read to relax. I got too relaxed and dozed off, only to be awakened out of a twilight sleep by my phone ringing. Answering in a daze, I didn't expect this. "Hello."

"Hello…this is Rikers Island, and you have a collect call from…" I sit up in a frantic state, it's him. I have to get this done today.

"Yes, I do accept."

"What's up baby, you sound happy to hear from me today."

"Hi Andre. I am happy to hear from you ,but not for the reason you think."

"What are you talking about, and why are you calling me Andre? You only call me that when you are mad at me."

"I'm about to tell you and after today, I don't want you to call me anymore. I have to let the past with me and you be just that, the past. I find I can't move forward Andre and it not your fault, I have to end this because clearly you had no problem ending things."

"Whooaa…hold up. Is that how you saw it; that I didn't have a problem?", Lane I still love you."

"Dre! I found you in bed with another woman, in our bed, so to me, you ended it. That love shit you're talking about it just that; shit. How could you have done that to me? I was always there for you."

"Stop it Lane. You and I are talking about two different relationships. You may have thought you was there for me, but you wasn't. It was always work or Charmine, and don't forget about your boy Greg."

"Greg, what does he have to do with this, you know we was over long before we even hooked up."

"So you say. It wasn't over Lane. Whenever a man can call and you drop everything, that shit ain't over, and you did it to me once too many times. Therefore I decided I needed someone to spend time with me, that's when and only when I started fucking with Renee. I can't explain why I brought her home. Maybe subconsciously I wanted you to find out hoping you would feel my pain, but it backfired. I didn't think you was going to leave me."

"Dre, what did you think was going happen after I found you two like that. You knew me well enough to know I wouldn't have stayed." There was a long pause before Dre spoke again. "Is this new cat good to you?"

"I just met him, but yes; he is a good man and I know I could be happy with him." Dre's pause gets a little longer after my response. "Lane I never wanted to keep you from being happy. I know that you and I loved each other, but it wasn't the kind of love that was going keep us together for our silver anniversary or no shit like that. I think about you all the time, but it's because I miss the sex; the sex was bananas, but a true relationship has to be more than sex."

"Dre, thank you so much for this. You don't know how much easier you have made this for me. I know what you are saying is correct, I think I just needed to hear you say it. Until today I thought I was still in love with you."

"Why is that?"

"I just realized I was in love with our past and couldn't move forward because I was stuck in the past. so thank you. What are they saying about your case?"

"I can't talk to you over the phone about it, that's another reason why I've been calling you. I want to see you face to face. When is the next time you coming to see your moms and pops?"

"That's ironic. My mother hasn't been doing well lately, so I'm surprising them with a visit in a few weeks, plus it's my dad's birthday around that time."

"Cool, if you do…please check me. If only as a concerned friend and I'll tell you everything."

"Alright Dre, with what you've given me today, I promise I will do as least that much for you."

"Well you know where I'm at. I'll put you on my visitors list today. Hope to see you soon"

"Sure will Dre, see you soon." He disconnects first and I sat there a few minutes more, holding the phone and staring into space. I haven't had this much peace in a long time. I knew what Dre said was spot on. While we was together, it was a rollercoaster ride. We looked great, had a hell of a sex life and even had mad good times, but I knew Dre and I didn't have what my parents have. I've always longed for a relationship as solid and as strong as theirs.

Relay-tionships

Chapter Ten

I wanted to call Clay so badly, but I knew if I did, he'd question if I could be free of Dre in just one night, so I decided against it. I opted for something I hadn't done in a long time and that is to take care of, and enjoy me. It has always been someone or something that caused me to be placed on the back burner and this experience with Dre and Clay, I must learn from it before I lose myself in someone else. Still content with my decision to take the position that was offered. I would let Mr Wyatt know first thing Monday morning. I decided I'd go to dinner and take in a movie by myself, things I would have never considered to do on my own. I always had to call Char or Faizon, for me to hit the town.

The weekend came and went by before I knew it. Faizon gave me a nice surprise on Sunday by calling and telling me she was feeling better, and could be released as early as Thursday. That was great news and I knew my Monday would be great just by hearing about her progress. I woke up to another Monday, but it's different. I'm taking the CFP position and best of all Faizon will be home this week.

I walked into the bank, brand new attitude and shoes. I wanted to handle my business. I told Mr Wyatt that I felt honored and would love to have the position that he offered. I asked for just one stipulation and that was in a couple of weeks, I'd be permitted to have a week off to fly to New York to see my parents. He agreed without any reluctance, informing me that my new position would keep me extremely busy, so I should prepare to push my sleeves up when I returned. He informed me that the first stage of my career would be as a member of a client team staffing conference for securities investors and arranging registration statements. I wondered what had I gotten myself into, but I knew I could handle it. Mr Wyatt told me who he had in mind to fill my current position, and informed me I would help his candidate with the transition. I told him of course, and assured him that I would make the transition go as smooth as possible.

After meeting with Mr Wyatt, I immediately booked my flight home. I felt guilty that I haven't been home since I moved here ducking my past, but I was so excited at just the thought of seeing my parents, and quite honestly, Dre as well. I planned to keep my trip a surprise from my parents. Each time I spoke with them, I was bursting inside, knowing that I would not have to tell them to kiss each other for me, I'd be able to do it myself. The very next day, I started an array of positive new ventures to occupy my time. I learned several things about myself; I discovered I liked to garden, cook, and art and not just because it was the "in" thing to do. Nevertheless, and most importantly, I learned I truly enjoyed being by myself without needing a man. Now don't get me wrong, I missed the hell out of Clay but I was glad to realize that I missed him because he was a good person, we had a lot in common, and seemed to enjoy each others company, it wasn't just about sex. So I knew when I returned, he would be the first person I called. I was so busy with my new title at the bank, I haven't been able to visit Faizon in the hospital the last few days, but I was glad that she was being released tomorrow. I didn't want Mr Wyatt to think I was taking advantage of my new status, so I decided I would wait until after work to visit her at her parent's home. Char has been so busy herself, that she and I hadn't seen each other practically all week, but planned to see each other tomorrow at the Hill's home After work, I get some Chinese food to take home because I knew I was in for the night. After I ate my Chinese food, I went into a deep slumber, and prayed for a better tomorrow.

Today was so stressful at work, I almost locked myself in the vault, but I knew I had to keep it together. I still wanted to go see Faizon at her parents after work, go shopping to get my dad's birthday gift, and pick up a few trinkets for my mother. We had one more meeting before I left work, and as soon as Mr Wyatt said it was over, I sprinted for the door as if he yelled fire. I stopped by the bagel shop, grabbed a bagel and some juice as I feel my energy depleting before I head to Faizons. Coming out the bagel shop I noticed a new art supplies store, so I popped in, and grabbed some things; I think Faizon can use, to keep her mind and ideas fresh.

Char called me as I stepped out of the store and asked me was I still going to see Faizon. I informed her that I was on my way. I got to the Hills and was greeted by Mrs Hill at the door. She invited me into their lovely home and she showed me to the room where Faizon is staying. "Aahh Faizon, you're looking wonderful!" I say to her as I walked over to plant a kiss on her forehead. Her head was still very much bruised, but the swelling has gone down considerably. "Thank you, I feel wonderful. I know I still have a long way to go, but I really do feel good." I gave her the supplies I just brought and she sprung up in bed, like a child at Christmas. She looked over each item and instantly came up with creative shit she can do with it. I know she said she was doing fine and I wanted her to remain in that frame of mind, but I really had to know any news about Darnell and what's the latest on his ass. I tiptoed around the subject, dropping hints until she caught on and offered information.

"Lane..." she started slowly, "Darnell admitted to what he did to me...and the baby. He'll remain in custody until his court date, when he'll be sentenced, my mother has already started preparing her statement to the judge to ensure that he never gets out."

"Did they discuss a court date, because I really want to attend, I feel the need to express my feelings to the court as well. I agree with your mother, he's a menace and should never see daylight again." Faizon have now jumped onboard realizing he must pay the consequences, which is being replaced by her normal looks of pity for him, so this is a good sign that she is coming around. I hope now she can see he needs to get the book thrown at him. Faizon announced she wants to change the topic of discussion, and does so by focusing on her new art supplies. "Thank you for the art supplies, I can't wait to get back to work. The problem is, I know my parents. even with Darnell in jail they're still very nervous about me returning home. As it is; all of a sudden, my mother wants me to see a therapist to talk about the baby. I truly don't need a therapist, I just don't feel comfortable talking to them about it. My dad blows up every time Darnell's name is mentioned, and all my mother does is cry. They can't seem to wrap their heads around I'll be fine. I don't need, or want to talk to a stranger about something as personal as this. I have you and Charmine...by the way, where is she?"

"She should be here shortly." I replied. I sat in a comfortable chair and listened as Faizon opened up her soul to me. I could see she really wanted to let it out and like she said, why pay a therapist, when she had her loved ones to listen for free. Faizon continued to talk about her future plans, and how now she is even more determined to make it on her own. She knew her dad would go to any lengths to take care of her, but she had to prove this to herself. As she started to share with me the visions of some designs while she was in the hospital, Mrs Hill escorted Charmine to the back to join us. She breezed in the room like she doesn't have a care in the world, and is looking quite well. Mr Martin definitely agrees with her.

She waltzed over to Faizon presented her with the loveliest bouquet of flowers, and pinched me on my cheek. Her conversation remained proper while Mrs Hill is still in the room, asking us about our week and complimenting Faizon on how good she looks. As soon as Mrs Hill exited the room, she pulls up a chair like she was Boquisha, the ghetto roving reporter to talk about her week with Anthony. It was apparent that Faizon and I had been starving for affection in any form, because we couldn't wait to hear what the hell's been happening between the two of them. Charmine went on to tell us how they fucked in her truck, in his car, in the elevator, in his office. I was getting turned on just by listening to her excitement, and then she hit us with the bombshell. "Well ladies... you two know I've always told y'all, how you don't have to search for love, just let it happen and if it's right, it'll come to you. Well, that's exactly what's happened...Anthony and I are getting married." It got so quiet in the room, I heard my dad eating his oatmeal in Brooklyn. I didn't know how to respond or what to say. I definitely knew she was ecstatic by the smile that took her entire face hostage. She looked at Faizon, and me, like she was at a tennis match waiting for something, anything. "Well, why are y'all so quiet?" She asks. I cleared my throat and squeaked out "Congratulations," and Faizon echoed the same. Charmine remained seated and her smile have slid completely off her face. "I just shared with you the happiest news, besides Faizon being home from the hospital and that's all I get… thanks sis-tahs."

"No. Char, I'm happy; truly happy for you. I'm just shocked. I have so many questions for you."

"Me too," chimes Faizon in, "when did all of this happen?"

"This morning, he surprised me with this!" She pulled out this diamond that was clearly five carats or better. "I know what you are thinking, we haven't known each other that long and what about my job, etc, etc, but if you think about it, we've known each other for nearly two years. Within that time Anthony and I have played with the idea of us starting our own firm long before we started anything sexual. All I know is that I love him, he loves me, and I want to marry him."

I knew she was a good lawyer, but damn! The way she pleaded her case, I knew she was in love. I had not seen her this happy since Kamel. She has dated since him but it was for her own needs, she never allowed herself to get too involved. Yeah, I can say this is the happiest she have been in forever. And she will have my support one hundred percent. The same way she has always had my back; good, bad, or indifferent. With that, I bum-rushed her with a huge hug, kiss and a more sincere congrats.

"Okay, I'm back bitches! We have a lot to do, wait… how long do we have?" I asked.

"We haven't set a date yet, he just asked me this morning,

but as soon as I know, you'll know. One thing I know for sure is, I've already tried a winter wedding, and it literally got me nowhere, so it has to be spring." She got up from her chair walked and around the room, sprouted ideas of what church, where the reception would be held, would the wedding be in Atlanta or in New York? Her face changed in mid-sentence; she looked sullen, as she clasped her hands together and covered her mouth. She looked as if she is about to cry, when she looked into Faizon eyes. She took her hands from her mouth and went back to sit down directly in front of her. "Faizon...will you do me the honor of designing and making my dress?" Faizon's face turned pomegranate red and her eyes welled up with water. It took her a few minutes to collect herself before she spoke.

"I would love to make your dress, but are you sure; you can afford to have anyone design your dress. This is your wedding dress we're talking about."

"You're so right. I can have anyone make my dress, but you're not just anyone. You're family." I sat back in my chair and watched the two of them touched to tears myself, secure in the fact, that moments like this will be forever cherished. Charmine leaned over the bed and nearly crushed Faizon with her weight, to get a hug. Mrs Hill entered the room and asked us what is with all the excitement back here. Faizon took the liberty to tell her mom that not only is Charmine getting married, but also she has asked her to make her wedding dress.

Mrs Hill grabbed Charmine, and placed a kiss on her cheek. "You've been so good to my daughter, husband and I. Please allow us the joy of hosting your rehearsal dinner. With your parents, living out of state and me knowing more than a few upscale venues it will be our pleasure, and one less thing your parents will have to stress over. Charmine accepted the more than gracious invitation and informed Mrs Hill that the only thing she knows for sure is that she wanted a spring wedding. She told Mrs Hill that a date haven't been set, but she will let her know as soon as she and Anthony have set one. Char expressed she knew the venues had to be booked well in advance, especially for a spring wedding which was soon approaching.

Mrs Hill offered us something to eat and drink before she left the room. We both declined but for different reasons. I was about to leave; my new position was already kicking my ass, plus I wanted to get some shopping done for my parents. Charmine announced that as of today she have put herself on a strict diet. As I prepared to leave, I apologized to Charmine for my initial reaction and reminded Faizon about the new art store very near my job, so if she wanted anything else to just let me know. Charmime decided she would stay awhile longer, so she and Faizon could toss some ideas around about her wedding and reception dresses. I told them happy designing and I'd talk to them later.

Relay-tionships

Chapter Eleven

On the way home I had a strong urge to call Clay. Just seeing, and hearing about how happy Charmine is, I knew I wanted to feel that way about someone. I fought back the urge and decided I would stick with my original plan and call him after I got back from New York. I left the mall dead tired after ordering my dad's birthday gift to be delivered to his door on his birthday and my mother a nice suit and hat for church. I couldn't wait to get home. I hopped in my car and thought how nice it would have been to have Clay's driver right about now.

I got home, showered, and headed straight for bed. I was in the best sleep I've had in weeks when my phone starts ringing. I was so sleepy; I thought I was dreaming until my cell starts ringing too. I picked up my phone groggy as hell; I know I must have sounded like Weezy Jefferson. I darted my eyes to my clock, and its 2:30 in the morning.

"Hel-loo."

"Lane…is this you…?" I must be dreaming. It sounds like

Clay's voice on the other end. God please, if this is a dream, it's a cruel one. I shook myself, nope I'm awake.

"Lane… this is Clay, I'm sorry for calling you at this hour."

"No Clay its fine. How are you, is everything okay?"

"No Lane, everything is not okay, because you're not lying beside me. I made a big mistake by letting you walk out my door and I've been regretting it ever since." I'm fully awake now and my palms started to sweat as he continued to talk to me. "I apologize for the way I showed you the door the last time we were together, I just can't apologize for why I did it." I sat and listened to his every word without interruption. I just loved the sound of his voice and it took everything in my power not to beg him to come over. "Listen," he continued, "I know it's late and you have to get up early, so can I see you tomorrow. We can finish this conversation then, if you say no I'll understand."

"Of course you can, it'll be after six before I can leave work. Will that work for you?"

"That's great, there's this little restaurant off Amsterdam Avenue I think you'll like. I'll call you later on today with all of the details and Lane…I'm looking forward to seeing you."

"Same here Clay, talk to you later, Goodnight."

"Goodnight Lane, sweet dreams." He hung up and I am stunned by what has just happened. That means he's been missing and thinking about me; just as much as I, him. You damn right sweet dreams; it can't get any sweeter than this and who in the hell can sleep now? What is it that he wants to say to me? I got out of bed and changed my entire outfit for tomorrow. I'm so glad I decided to get my hair done. I gave my outfit one more glance over and hit the bed for real now. I know I'm going to be tired as hell at work today, but it sure will be worth it. I laid there in anticipation of my alarm going off. As soon as I saw the sunlight through my window, I hopped up without the alarm. Today was a new day and I was ready to greet it. I couldn't have been at work an hour when Clay calls to give me the details of where we are meeting. I made it through work without completely going bonkers. All I seemed to be doing so far is being held in the longest and drawn out meetings. Finally, I wrapped up the last meeting of the day with my team and head out to meet my Clay.

I called him when I approached the restaurant only for him to tell me he's already inside. I sashayed inside the restaurant and he's waiting for me at our table. I took one look at him and melted. He looked splendid. He stood up and welcomed me to our table with a quick kiss, and embraced me with his stanch arms. He released me and I sat across from him and just imagined us in a world where no-one else exists. The waiter came over and brought us water and our menus; he asked if we were ready to order. Clay told him we'll start with drinks, gives him our order and the waiter disappeared. I had butterflies as I waited for him to start. He reached across the table and caressed my face with his masculine hands before he spoke.

"Lane... I missed you." I took his hands in mine, kissed, and held on to them as I responded.

"I missed you too, how have you been?"

"Like I told you last night not good, I haven't stopped thinking about you from that night. Lane, I started to tell you last night why I couldn't apologize for why I made the move I did." He paused while he waited for the waiter to serve our drinks before he continued. Clay asked him to give us a little more time to consider our food order. The waiter nodded and vanished to serve another table. Clay returned his full attention back on me. "I want you to know that, I want you in my life and the reason I can't apologize for why I asked you to leave is because, I can't have you if you are involved with someone else." I stopped him before he proceeded to say anything further.

"Clay, I told you I haven't seen Dre since I left New York and that's been almost two years."

"Wait Lane, let me finish. I know you said you haven't been with him physically in two years, but I'm talking about emotionally. You got to understand something, I'm a man, and when a man has your emotions, it's only a matter of time before he can have you physically, so that's why I stressed to you that I need you to be sure you're free, completely free of Dre, not just physically, but emotionally as well."

"You mean want don't you?" He thought about what he said and gave me a smile that lit my soul.

"You're right, I need and want you. Is that better?"

"Yes, that's much better. Now may I tell you something?" He sat back and took a sip of his drink before I spoke. I felt like this was do or die, so I chose my words very carefully, because I wanted to convey to him that I wanted him just as much without sounding needy. "When you asked me about my feelings for Dre that evening, I was still confused and it wasn't until I left your house, thinking that I may still have something for him. Possibly even be still in love with him, until I spoke to Dre. Instead what I discovered was that I was in love with a past. With memories that could not be shared with my grandchildren because, they were based on sex. I want to have memories on things I'm proud of, of what me and my partner have built together. Like my parents, I envy them and they don't even know it. I know what they have been through, and they love each other more now than they did when they got married."

"That's what's up, now I can respect that and that's exactly what I'm talking about for me…and you if you want it. What I'm saying is this. I want to build our own memories, but I want a clean slate to build a foundation, and it can't be like that with lingering memories from your past." The waiter returned for our order and while Clay is ordering, I decided to let him know of my trip home and my intentions to see Dre for the last time. The waiter took our order and was gone again. Once he was completely out of earshot, I informed Clay that I will be leaving for home next week and that I would be seeing Dre during my visit. He folded his arms and rested his body caddy cornered of our booth. Never taking his eyes off me, he asked why did I have to see him. I told him that Dre and I resolved our issues over the phone and how we both came to the realization that our relationship was doomed from the start because it was based solely on sex. I assured him that my visiting Dre was me merely extending my hand to a friend who was in trouble. He shook his head full of well-groomed loc's and said he trusted me to do what was right.

"There was something else I wanted to talk to you about. When are you coming back from New York? I have a surprise for you."

"I'll be there for a week, so I'll be back in Atlanta on the fifteenth."

"Great, you will be back in time!"

"In time for what?" I yelled.

"I said a surprise. Don't worry, you'll enjoy it."

"How do you know I'll enjoy it?" Hoping he would question, if I would like it or not and tell me, but he didn't take the bait.

"Because I pay attention and that's all you need to know.

181

Plus here's our food." I was so happy to be with him, I couldn't eat. I just forked over my food, but I watched him eat and wished he would devour me the way he was his steak. I wanted to get out of there, before I let my guard and panties down. It wouldn't take much to suggest he follows me home. So far I was doing well by not undressing him right there at our table. I just needed to see if I could suppress my sexual urges, to now start building the relationship, like the one we both just spoke of.

While we ate, he asked me what I had been up to. I told him about my new position at the bank, about Faizon being out of the hospital and Charmine getting engaged. He congratulated me on my new position by rubbing my inner thigh from under the table. He grinned as he told me he knew where to go, if his company ever needed any money and added he was happy that my girls were good. We finished our food and he paid the bill. He thanked me for joining him for dinner and helped me up from the table. When we got outside, he walked me to my car and he asked me would we see each other before I flew out. I told him I hoped that we would.

"What are you doing this weekend?"

"Probably nothing."

"Would you like to do probably nothing with me?" I laughed and told him yes.

"I'll call you later Clay." The way we kissed and groped each other in the parking lot of the restaurant, we might have well have gone to his house, but instead, he opened my car door, and knelt down to put my seatbelt on. "I can't have anything happen to you." He kissed me one last time and watched me as I drove off. I commended myself for not fucking him in my backseat, but I can't help but play over in my head what we just talked about. Now he has a surprise for me, what could it be?

I marveled at the possibilities. I know we have basically just met, but I do believe in love at first sight. All the way home, I busted my brain trying to guess what the surprise could possibly be that would await my return to Atlanta. I felt so charged just knowing that I will be with him this weekend, and since I'll be gone the following week, I'll fuck him for time lost and get some for reserve.

What a week, it's had some ups and downs, but mainly good; and I thanked God that Faizon is home. I reminded myself I need to get a victim's statement prepped for Faizon's case against Darnell. I pray the judge will hear us and sentence him to the max. In thinking about Charmine and Faizon, I recalled what Dre said to me about being so involved in everyone else's life, that he felt neglected and I want to make sure that history doesn't repeat itself with Clay. I will have to devise a balance, which will prevent the same thing from reoccurring. I truly want to make this work.

Saturday morning came, and Clay kept his promise and came over for breakfast. He asked me to get some things to take back to his house for the weekend, because he has a slew of new unsigned talent. He is confident that at least three are promising and he wants to sign at least one of the artists before they scout other labels. He didn't talk much about his work, but I knew he took it very serious. I listened to how he would jump in his folks' ass about being lackadaisical and remind them if he doesn't make money; they don't make money. After I tidied up and got my weekender packed, Clay and I headed for his house. I get to see his entire gorgeous house this visit and this time he takes my bag straight upstairs to his room. Clay showed me what he felt I would need to be familiar with; the numbers to the markets that delivered and how to operate all of his gadgets in his living room before he disappeared to his studio. He told me to make myself at home and left me in the great room while he immediately started making calls.

He stayed in his studio most of the day with his potential new artists, and team. I occupied my time with three-way calls to Charmine and Faizon, listening to them talk about the many ideas they have come up with for Charmine's wedding gown. Just hearing about the detailing of the fabric and style, I knew it would be exquisite and Charmine will look exquisite in it. While I talked to my girls, I showed off my newfound culinary skills and fixed us some shrimp and steak skewers. I dressed it up with a hearty salad and chilled white wine. Clay came upstairs periodically to grab some food and my ass, and went right back downstairs to finish this track with this new rapper he said was sic on the mic. I felt privileged to meet him, that when he goes platinum, I can say I knew him when. By the time Clay finished with his folks, I had showered and was upstairs watching TV.

After the tracks were finished, he came upstairs, complimented me on my cooking, and hopped in the shower. When he stepped out, he was butt-ass naked; my eyes couldn't help but be drawn to his manhood that was erected like a sculptured, fine piece of art. Speechless, Clay eased onto his bed, pulled my panties off, and put his mouth on my pussy with such tenderness it sent me into another dimension. I felt as though I was having an outer body experience. Even the touch of his wooly loc's between my thighs felt magnificent. By the time he entered me, I already had two orgasms. I was thrilled about how we spent our weekend. When Clay took me home on Sunday, I had accomplished just what I set out to do and that was to fuck us into a reserve that would be sufficient until I got back from New York.

Each day I got more and more excited to see my parents.

One night I almost gave my secret away when my mother told me she wasn't feeling well and I told her I would talk to her doctor when I got there, but I recovered quickly because my mother didn't question what I had said. Clay and I were so busy the week I was to leave, we saw each other only once but he scheduled a car to take me to the airport. My flight was for 8 a.m., so it was so nice to open my front door the morning of and see a car waiting to whisk me off to Hartsfield International. I boarded the plane and put my eye shields on. By the time I took a quick snooze and read a magazine my flight was landing at JFK. I scurried to get my bags and hailed a taxi to get me to my parents' house. As we approached the old neighborhood, memories started to flood my mind.

I know I've only been gone two years but everything looked so different, they built a couple of new stores on the block; a convenience store and a Chicken and Rib shack, which I know my dad kept them in business. I hurried out of the taxi, while the driver got my luggage out of his truck. I'm nervous and don't know why, I thanked the driver for getting my bags and head to the door. I rang the doorbell three times before my parents even asked who it was. Finally, I heard footsteps.

"Who is it?"

"It's me daddy." When he hears "daddy," all I hear is him fumbling to get the door open in a panic and calling for my mother.

"Lynn... Lynn, Lord have mercy. It's our baby!" By the time he got the door opened, my mother has put her bathrobe on and has met us at the door with opened arms. "Lane you angel. Come on in here baby and let us look at you." My mother yanked me in the house and hugs me so tightly, I heard her bones creek. My dad stood back and watches us with an it's my turn to love her up look in his eyes. Mommy reluctantly let me

185

go and dad picked up where she left off. He released his hug but continued to hold me by both of my shoulders, and stood me in front him.

"Why didn't you tell us you was coming? I could've picked you up from the airport."

"No, I wanted this to be a surprise; I didn't want you and mommy to go to any trouble." My mother had sat down in her lazy girl chair and asked how I could ever be any trouble. I knew I haven't seen my mother in close to two years; but she looked so thin, almost weak. I'm so glad I'm home; first thing today we are making an appointment to see her doctor. I joked with dad about his upcoming birthday and getting older. I asked him would he like to invite Moses to his party and he belted out this hearty laugh, which caused his eyes to water. I knew my dad loved me because each birthday I repeated the same wack ass joke, and he cracked up like it was fresh material.

"Ma, how are you doing…really?"

"Precious, you're here now, so I can't hide it. I haven't been doing so well; I have been feeling weaker by the day." I instantly have a talk with myself. Lane stay composed, you don't want your parents to see you fall apart in the first ten minutes of your visit. Just swallow and take a deep breath. I followed my own instructions, before I spoke.

"Ma, why haven't you told me this before now?" My voice is cracking every other word.

"Cause sweetheart, your dad and I thought it was best not to disturb you with our problems. You're living in Atlanta now, on top of an extremely demanding role at your job. It was just better this way." I felt horrible, listening to the reasons that my mother voiced that they felt they couldn't tell me, and who was to blame. It was I, who chose not to come home in so long because of my issues with Dre. How could I let that keep me from visiting my parents? I couldn't bear to hear anymore so I cut her off. "Ma, I told you hundreds of times never keep anything from me, especially when it comes to your health. If I lived in Timbuktu it wouldn't matter, I'll be here and about the matter of my job demanding or not you're my mother. You'll always come first!" My dad had sulked in his lazy boy chair and looked down at his feet.

"What time does your doctor's office open this morning?"

"He's already opened." Dad answered in a hush tone. Still looking at his feet, almost as if he felt ashamed by keeping this all a secret from me. I scrolled through my phone, found his office number, and connected the call.

"Hello, Dr. Abraham's office."

"Hi, this is Lane King, Mrs King's daughter. My mother isn't feeling so well today and I would like to schedule an appointment for her to be seen at the next earliest appointment; today if possible please."

"Hold please while I check to see what he has available."

"Yes, I'll hold" While I'm on hold my body is sobbing from head to toe, just thinking of how my mother needed me and I'm less than three hours away. I had no idea how sick she was getting again. The nurse returned to the line and informs me that the earliest would be tomorrow morning at 8:45. I assured her that we will be there. I also asked her to make a notation for the doctor to allot some extra time for this appointment as I wanted to ask some questions and I don't want to be rushed out because of some mandatory fifteen minutes timeslot bullshit. I started to unpack and I gave my mother her gifts which she absolutely adored. She promised that she would be wearing her new hat and suit this Sunday. "Thanks baby, I can just see Sister Johnson's face now." My mother amused herself with the thought of her church sisters' jealousy. I gave my dad part one of his gift and told him part two will be here the morning of his birthday. He opened the box and was obviously pleased with the golf attire he just received. He said the next time he went to the course, he would look better than Tiger Woods himself. Little did he know he had some new clubs being delivered Wednesday morning to complete his birthday gift. I asked them who was attending dad's shindig. My mother grunted as she mentioned my Aunt Bernice on my dad's side was coming with her clan as she calls them. "Lane, we're expecting all your uncles, a few of the church members and some of your dads retired buddies. Oh yeah your cousin Beverly will be here too." Oh great, I really want to see her and ask why she felt it necessary to pass my number out to Dre. My mother interrupts my thoughts with her mentioning she was cooking all the food.

"I have to pick up some chickens. I'll need to have them cleaned before hand, so I don't have to worry about frying them at the last minute."

"You definitely won't be cleaning or frying any chickens. We're having daddy's party catered. First of all; you're not well, and secondly its daddy's sixtieth birthday and this is going to be sweet and pleasurable for all of us." I know it was going to be hard for my mother to sit back and allow someone else to cook for daddy's birthday bash, but no way was I going to permit her to be frying chicken and baking cakes all day in her condition. The first day I just chilled, and listened as ma called everybody and their friends, just to let them know her "baby" was in town. I laughed at my parents as I watched the two of them have major discussions about the news and weather. I thought was this what Clay and I had to look forward to. Just thinking about him; jarred my memory that he told me to call him when I got in. I excused myself from my parent's room and went into my old room and called him. He picked up on the first ring, "What's up Lady, are you there yet?" I didn't realize that when I heard his voice, I would get a rush of emotions that caused me to breakdown"

"Hello Clay, yes I'm here."

"Baby... what's the matter, is your moms alright?"

"No Clay, she isn't alright and I'm scared for her."

"Lane, I'm sorry to hear that. If there's anything I can do, you know what to do."

"I know and thank you for that. I just needed to hear your voice. I'm sorry; I didn't intend to call you while I was in such a state."

"Come on stop that; you never have to apologize for that. When did you say your dad's birthday was again?"

"It's Wednesday, but we are having his party on Friday."

"Cool, are you going to be alright."

"Yeah, I'll be fine. It's just that seeing my mother this way was too much for me."

"No doubt, I know this might be the appropriate time to bring this up, but are you still planning to see Dre?"

"Yes Clay, I thought we resolved that and you felt..."

"Yeah we did. I just wanted to see if you have a change of heart."

"Clay, if you don't want me to then I won't."

"No, do what you gotta do. I'm good, like I said I trust you will do what's best for all concerned."

"Thanks Clay, I do need to do this, not even for us, but for me."

"Alright, on a lighter note I signed the R&B and the rap

artist this morning."

"Who Sammy G?"

"Yeah, I told you he's sic with his lyrics."

"I'm so happy for you."

"Nah be happy for us." We continued to talk about a few things we were going to do when I got back to Atlanta. I tried to get him to tell me about my surprise, but he was serious about keeping it under wraps. He said he had some calls he needed to take, but told me he would arrange my pick up from the airport, when I returned. I was so glad I spoke to him. I felt much calmer and I was thrilled about him signing the new artists. I went back into the room with my parents, my mother asked me about Charmine and if I made any other good friends since I've been in Atlanta. I told her about Faizon and her ordeal with Darnell, and Charmine's engagement. She was thrilled to hear about Charmine's second chance at happiness, but she was worried when I mentioned Faizon's dilemma and begged me to please make sure that I always locked my doors. My dad suggested that I learn how to shoot and get a license to carry a gun. My mother got on to my dad for even making that suggestion.

I don't know if my mother was forcing herself to do things since I was there, but she appeared to look a little better by dinner time. That night before my head touched my pillow I prayed that God put a special blessing upon my mother. I needed her, and I know my dad needed her even more. Seeing my mother like this has forced me to re-think my future plans.

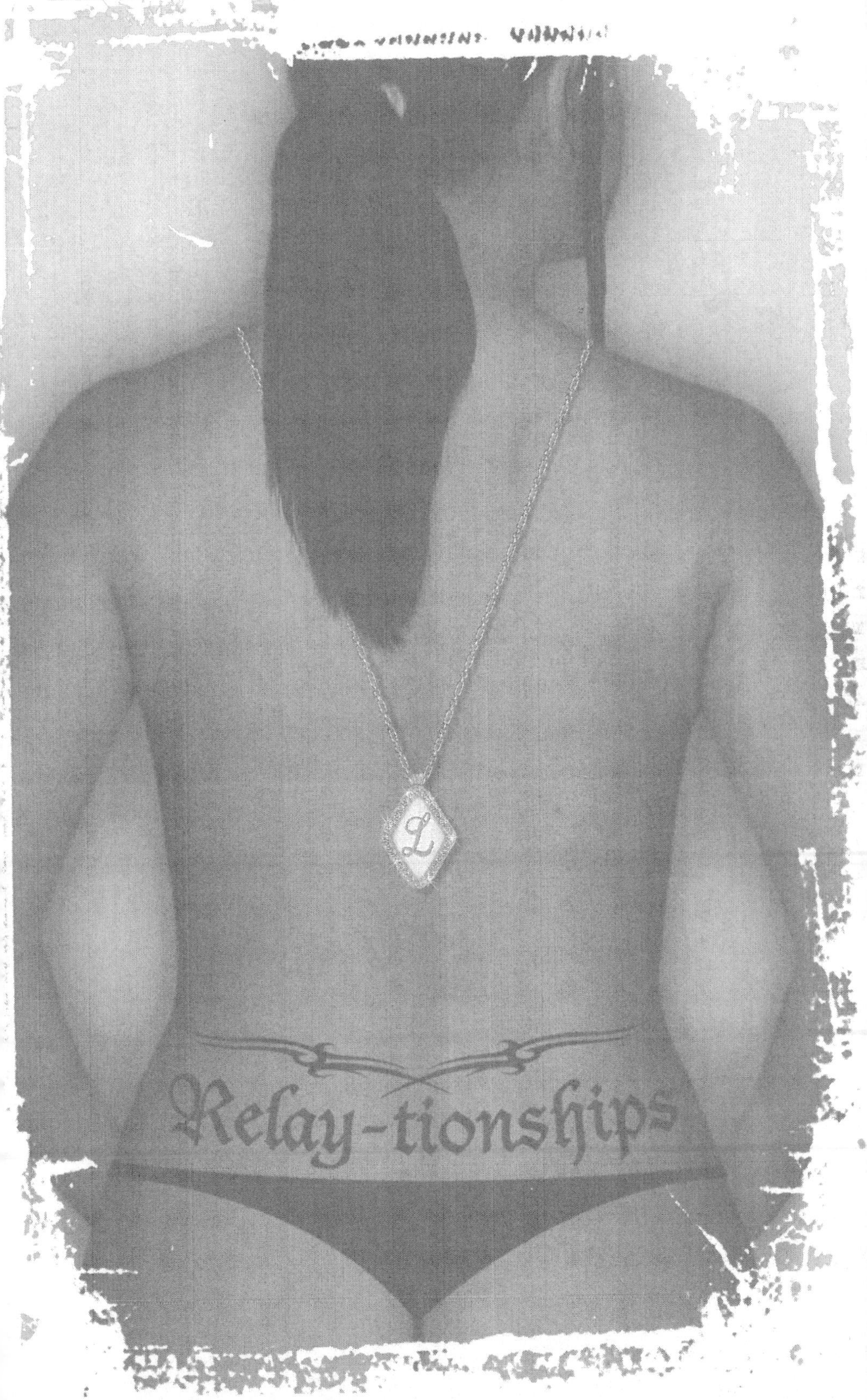
L
Relay-tionships

Chapter Twelve

The next morning, I awoke to the smell of fresh coffee, bacon and eggs. I went out to say good morning and both my parents are fully dressed, at seven in the morning; looking at them made me feel lazy. I ate my breakfast before I got dressed and mentally prepared myself for my mother's doctor's appointment. I grabbed all my mother's medicines, while my dad walked her to the car. We arrived at Dr. Abraham's office and while dad parked the car; my mom and I walked in. As we walked into the doctor's office the nurse's eyes meet my mothers and asked her to come straight to the back for her weight and blood pressure. I followed them as the nurse led the way.

"Good morning Mrs King. I'm sorry you're not feeling well today. Who have you brought with you today?"

"This is my daughter Lane, she lives in Atlanta and she surprised us with a visit on yesterday." I greeted the nurse and thanked her for fitting my mother in so quickly. "No problem, your mother is one of our favorites patients." After the cordial chit-chat, the triage nurse directs us to a room. My dad has now joined us in the room and starts to skim through a magazine. We're in the room only a short time before Dr. Abrahams knocked on the door before he entered the small examining room. He is a tall, attractive man with a strong presence. He said hello while he placed his hand on my mother's shoulder. He looked in my direction and extended his hand for me to shake as we introduced ourselves. He announced that he heard my mother wasn't doing too well and ordered for her to have some blood work and some x-rays done. I reminded him that I wanted him to answer a few of my questions. He said he would be more than happy to, but asked if I could wait until the lab and x-rays came back he would be better able to answer any questions I may have for him.

Dr. Abrahams asked my mother what has been going on since her last appointment, she expressed that she has been feeling weak and all of her joints have been aching terribly. The doctor took notes as my mom talked. After he checked her from head to toe, he calls for the same, kind nurse to escort my mother to the lab and x-rays. In my mother's absence, my dad told me how happy he is to see me and how much this means to him and mother. "I love your mother very much, she's had my heart from the day I saw her at the malt shop in town. I knew right then she would be my wife." Listening to him, I figured out maybe that's why I believe in love at first sight. "I know you love her daddy, she's going to be fine." I don't know who needed to hear that more, him or me. We laughed at how his party was going to be a trip knowing how mommy couldn't stand my Aunt Bernice. Mommy felt she was always trying to "take over." "Don't worry dad, I will referee." We were still laughing about it, when ma walked back in the room. "What are you two laughing about?" I lied and told her I was envisioning Uncle Snuck dancing at the party. My mother believed me, because dad backed me up and ma knows Uncle Snuck can't dance. We waited patiently in our room, but I did notice that it was taking a considerably long time waiting on the doctor to bring back the results. I took that time to use the restroom and when I got back the doctor was already in the room waiting on me now. The doctor asked me to take a seat that he had the nurse bring in. Dr. Abrahams tone was more subdued than it was before, which gave me a bad vibe and with what he said next, my feelings were accurate. Mrs King, I regret telling you that your x-rays shows several spots of cloudiness, which tells me the cancer has returned and spread. Come on God, what kind of cruel shit is this. My heart is racing and my body temperature has risen, as I listened to the doctor explain his findings.

I looked in my mother face trying to read any emotion, but she had no expression at all, and my dad got up and stared at the x-rays the doctor has displayed for us, as if he was praying it belonged to someone else. The doctor asked if we had any questions. I had tons of questions I prepared for him yesterday, but they all seem to escape me now, because the only question I care to get an answer to is, is my mother going die and since I can't hear anything other than a convincing NO, I tell him I have no questions. Dr. Abrahams talks to my mother about her medicines being changed and she'll have to start back with her chemotherapy. He assured us that he would make himself available if we needed to talk or have any questions. I thanked him and we sat in room waiting on the nurse to bring us the new prescriptions and information about when my mother will resume her treatments.

After the nurse went over the details with us, she wished us luck and said it was nice meeting me. It was at that precise moment, I knew what had to be done. I was coming home again. I would go back to Atlanta long enough to tie up some loose ends, and say good bye to the one man I felt would love me unconditionally. The rest of the day was miserable, I called Char and told her what the doctor findings was. She and I cried together, she really lost it when I told her I was moving back home. She tried to persuade me not to make such a rushed decision.

"Lane, I can't imagine what you must be feeling, so I won't try; but I know your mother and she wouldn't want you to leave the life you've built here. You've got your dream house, dream career, and now man."

"I know Char; you don't think I've thought about all of that. It kills me, for once I feel a true chance at happiness, but none of the above is more precious than my mother."

"I don't want to sound selfish, what about me? I'm in Atlanta because of you."

"Well in that case, you should be thanking me every time you look at that rock on your finger. Don't forget, I'm not the only one who found my dream man. All I know is that here is where I'm needed."

"Have you told Clay yet?"

"No! I haven't talked to him today and I don't intend to tell him something of this magnitude over the phone," I had to change the subject, "how is Faizon, I called her yesterday but no one was home?"

"Actually she is doing terrific. She had her first appointment yesterday and everything is getting back to normal, she even went to pick up some fabric for my dress. My Dress, will you be here for my wedding?"

"Bitch, you talking crazy now, of course I'll be there for

your wedding, listen let me get off this phone, I need to get this food ordered for dad's party."

"I'm glad you didn't cancel and thanks for inviting my parents. My mother said she can't wait to see you."

"Me too, my dad and I tried to cancel, but ma wasn't having it. Anyway, call me tomorrow and tell Anthony I said hello."

"I will, and kiss your parents for me." We disconnected and I thought about what Char said. Honestly, leaving my job and selling my house was the easy part, but Clay, he wasn't as easy for me to come to grips with, but if he wants me as he says he does, we can have a long distance relationship. Who knows, maybe he'll even consider moving here. I went to check on my mother and she's resting comfortably. While my mother rested, I took the opportunity to talk one-on-one with my dad about my decision. I walked in on my dad watching the news, and before I can ask if I can talk to him, he turns off the TV. "Dad, I want you and ma to know I'm sorry about not coming home more often. It must have been hard on you taking care of mommy while she was sick all by yourself, but I want you to know this time it will be different." I pause before I finished my sentence because I knew once I put it out there, I can't take it back. My dad sat still and waited for me to continue, "This time you'll have help...daddy, I am moving back to New York." My dad sat back in his chair and folded his arms. "Lane, I don't want you to think I don't appreciate the unselfish act you're prepared to do. I don't even want you to think I don't want you to move back here, because I would love having both my angels here with me, but please, don't move back if your reasoning is you'll feel guilty. I know as you got older you felt it was necessary to look after us, but I made a vow to look after my wife, your mother, for better and for worse."

"I know daddy, and I'm not saying you can't do it. I just

want to help you and ma through this."

"What, do you think we'll love, or think of you any less if you continue to live your life in Atlanta, a fruitful life I might add? Listen to me Lane, what do you think your mother is going to say. Do you think she would want you to let go of your life to take care of us? Lane, I know you want to do what is right but, The Lord is my Shepherd. You keep moving around for the wrong reasons. You left here running away from something or someone and if you come back, although you think it's for the right reason, pretty soon you'll regret it. Guilt has a way of turning into resentment and before you know it you'll be miserable and me and your mother love you too much to allow that to happen to you."

"Daddy, I will take into account what you've said, but I've already made up my mind. I'm moving back. I have enough in my savings to get me through, until I find a job here and I can get a small apartment close to you. I'll be fine."

"I hear what your mouth is saying, but do yourself a favor and think it through."

"I love you daddy, but I have thought about it." And with that I went into my room and started drafting my resignation on my laptop. I figured I will need a month to coordinate my move. That meant I could give Mr Wyatt, at least a three-week notice. Just thinking about leaving my job, a tiny wave of sadness infused my body and that was just thinking about my job. How was I going to feel leaving Clay. Clay called me right as I was going to bed that night, he told me how badly he missed me already and coerced me into having phone sex with him. He told me to just imagine the real thing when I got home. I didn't have the heart to even broach the subject of me moving back home. The next morning as promised the golf shop delivered my dad's clubs for his birthday. My mother and

I sang happy birthday to my dad as he ate his favorite breakfast. We watched him swing his new clubs on an imaginary green in our living room. The first call my dad got from one of his buddies, he invited them to the golf course for eighteen holes. He asked us if we minded; if he left us for the day to play some golf. We told him to go and enjoy his day. This was the first time my mother and I was alone since my visit and I was looking forward to it. We talked and laughed about silly stuff, she told me how she still watched "OPRAH TV SHOW" every day and how Oprah had a show on children reversing roles with their parents. I knew this was a segue about the conversation I had with my dad, about me moving home.

"Baby... my mother started sweetly, "your dad told me what you are planning to do, and I think that is the sweetest thing, but can I be honest with you."

"Of course ma, I want you to."

"I love you and want nothing but the best for you, but I don't want you to move back home. I know this may sound silly, but I can't be sick with you here. I will always feel like I have to be up doing something to make you feel better, do you understand that."

"Yes, a little bit, but it's not about me reversing my role or as daddy thinks; feeling guilty. This is something I need to do and with all due respect ma, I've made up my mind. You and daddy should just resolve the fact that I'll be here next month for good." My mother looked at me and realized that I was serious, and we moved to another subject. The day went well and I still had some unfinished business with Dre and I wanted to get that over and done with before my dad's party. I planned my visit with Dre for Thursday. I feel a little out of place visiting a jail so I called my cousin Beverly who appears to enjoy the life style of visiting her man in jail, and just as I suspected she tells me she'll be more than happy to pick me up.

The next day Beverly picked me up as promised. I told my parents that we'll be back later in the afternoon. No sooner than Bev and I are alone, I asked her what possessed her to give my number to Dre, without at least consulting me first. Her excuse was that he had thrown her off guard. She was there visiting her boyfriend and there was Dre, visiting with his girlfriend, so she didn't think anything of it. I told her to just forget it, what's done is done.

We got to the jail and I felt humiliated. I felt as if I were the criminal. I was searched, stripped of my cell phone, perfume and my pride. I sat in a room until they called our names one by one, and in no particular order. I sat at this metal table and waited for Dre to come from the back. I sat and watched as a string of good looking brother's kept marching out to greet their loved ones. Some were their mothers, but the majority were girlfriends and baby mamas undoubtedly vowing to put their lives on hold until their men got their shit together. One by one, they passed my table and undressed me with their eyes. One dude was bold enough to flat out stare at me to the point his girl had to physically turn his face back in her direction. Beverly warned me in advance so, I put a lot of thought in my attire to make sure I didn't dress to provocatively. After so many lewd looks and comments I realized, I could have worn a turtleneck, it wouldn't have made any difference, these were men behind the wall. After I felt violated by one inmate, who held his dick while eyeing me, Dre finally walks out. Shit, I had forgotten how good he looked. He approached me and before I could object, his tongue was in my mouth. I reciprocated, until the butch looking female guard yelled "No touching" from across the room. I wondered if the guard hadn't stopped us, would I have continued to allow Dre to kiss me that way.

200

I'm so confused but as the visit progressed, I knew that kiss, neither Dre meant anything to me.

"Damn, you still look good as hell Lane."

"Thanks... so do you considering. How have you been holding up?"

"I'm good. I prefer to be home though, but this is home for me right now."

"So what are they saying, are they focusing on you only... what?"

"My court appointed attorney says I have a good chance of beating it, but that's just it, he's court appointed."

"Why don't you think you have a good shot with him, especially if he's hopeful about your case?" Dre looked at me and laughed.

"Lane, you're still so naïve. I guess that'll never change." I sat across from him dumbfounded. Was that a diss he just issued, and if it is; I need to let him know I won't tolerate it.

"Well if I'm so fucking naive, why did you have to see me in person? What was so important that you couldn't tell my naive ass over the phone?"

"Renee and I was thinking..."

"Wait ...you and who?"

"Renee, my girl you remember."

"Dre, don't play me! You know good and fucking well I remember the bitch. I thought you told me a couple of weeks ago you two were through. You know what... this is my fault. I don't know why I keep letting you fuck with my brain."

"Hold up, wasn't you the same one a couple of weeks ago thanking me for setting yo ass free... wait Lane, I'm sorry... I didn't ask you here for this."

"So what did you ask me here for?"

"If you allow me to finish, I'm gonna tell you. We was hoping that you would give me the money for a good lawyer, or maybe your girl Charmine could represent me." Now it's my turn to laugh. I laughed myself to tears. I even leaned in closer to Dre, so he can hear my every word. "Are you out of your fucking mind? You were "going to tell me." How dare you even suggest that I loan you, let alone give you as much as a penny! Furthermore, do you really believe that Charmine would represent your ass after the way you treated me. Wait, I got a better plan, how about you and that mud-duck of a ho ass bitch come up with the dough yourselves, and if y'all can't… don't drop the soap."

Humiliation caused me to storm out of the visitor's area. I was blind with anger, but I could still hear some of the prisoners hissing and yelling out their inmate numbers at me. I ignored all of my jailhouse propositions and headed straight for Beverly's car. I didn't even stop by the front to pick up my belongings. I needed to get some air first. I'll just wait for Beverly to finish with her visit and then I'll go back in and get my phone and other property. When Beverly got out, I was still fuming, the nerve of him. I collected myself long enough to go back inside, gather my items and run back to the car without turning back.

Today I'm officially free from that bastard. Beverly dropped me off at my parents. I asked her if she wanted to come in. She told me she would, but she had so much to do today, especially now that Aaron her boyfriend added his to do-list. She would just see us tomorrow at my dad's party. I thanked her for taking me to hell, she laughed and sped off. I entered the house and my mother is getting things prepared for tomorrow's festivities. She stopped long enough to ask about Dre.

"Hey baby how did it go, Is he alright?" I lied through my teeth.

"Oh yeah ma; he's fine. His girlfriend is getting him a top notch lawyer so he shouldn't be in there too much longer." How could I tell her that he was just using me, but today was truly the last time.

"Charmine has been calling you all afternoon. She said she even tried your cell but it was turned off." I told my mother my phone was confiscated during my visit with Dre. I rushed to return her call, but now her voicemail is on. I hoped everything was alright. I hadn't spoken to Faizon since I have been here and decided to give her a call.

"Hello."

"Hello Faizon, how are you?"

"Lane... hi. I'm doing wonderful. Good to hear your voice; Char told me you tried to call; I've been busy as a bee."

"That's great news, so how is everything coming along?"

"Productive, I've found the material for Char's dress and she loves it. She's going to look what I want to call "beautifully classic". I wish you were here you could help me with some minor odds and ends; you have such great taste."

"Thanks, I'll be home on Sunday."

"Yeah; but for how long? Char told me of your plans to move back to New York. I'm sorry to hear about your mother. I wish there was something I could do. I know this has to be a difficult decision you're faced with, however: I will ask have you thought about commuting?"

"Yes I have, and I just feel it's best for all of us this way."

"It sounds like you thought it out. I must tell you, I want to thank you for being there for me when my parents and me needed you Lane. You've encouraged me so much to continue my fashion line and I'm about to show the world what I have to offer."

"I know you are and I can't wait to wear your designs." We laughed a few minutes more about trivial stuff before hanging up.

My parents went to bed early in anticipation of my dad's party. I continued to try to reach Char without success. I even called Clay to see if he wanted round two of some raunchy phone sex, but he didn't pick up either. Bored myself; I retired right along with my parents.

The day of the party, God blessed my dad with a beautiful February morning. It was a crisp cold day but the sun was shining so brightly. This time I was up and dressed before my parents got up, prepared a continental breakfast, and served them in bed. I made appointments for me and my mom to get our hair, nails and facials done. I hoped she would be up for it, especially since I haven't told her yet. My Aunt Bernice called and said she was coming over early to help out, so I knew that was a sure fire way that ma would get out of the house. My mother tried her hardest to dissuade her by telling her, that we had everything under control. It was like talking to a brick wall, my aunt kept insisting that there must be something she could do. When it was evident that my aunt was still coming hell or high water, it gave ma pleasure in telling her that we had a morning of beauty scheduled and wouldn't be here when she arrived. I reminded my dad to please make sure he is home for the caterers, which would be here promptly at four to start setting up and he promised he would.

My mother looked a little peaked but she fought through it. Once we arrived, Liz and her staff commenced with the pampering. My mother said she was so happy she decided to come; she could really use a facial. While my mother was getting her hair done, I thought I'd better call my dad and check on him and Aunt Bernice to see if the caterers had arrived. My dad told me the food hadn't come yet, but another package did. Knowing that dad had family from all over, I just assumed he was insinuating another birthday gift had arrived, and said that's nice.

I didn't want him to think that we deserted him, so I told him as soon as ma's hair was done; we're on our way home. He told us to take our time and enjoy the moment. With my mom's hair and facial done, she looked ten years younger. I now see where I get my beauty from. I hailed a taxi and we are on our way back home. As my mom and I entered our lovely brownstone, I hear my Aunt Bernice displaying her, come hither laugh and wondered who she is trying to impress.

I walked into the living room and there sits the absolute, most perfect, 6'1 chocolate specimen in Brooklyn, being entertained by my dad and aunt who continued to cackle. The second Clay saw me he pounced to embrace me. I buried my face in his strong chest and respired his essence. The moment seemed surreal, and we both were oblivious of our surroundings. While I held onto Clay and tuned the world out, my dad told my mother how he played a joke on me by omitting the fact that Clay was the package he boasted about arriving earlier. Being mindful of my parents and aunts presence, he kissed me lightly on my lips. My parents and Aunt Bernice dared to leave their places. He unleashed me long enough to be introduced to my mother.

"Ma, this is Clay, the man I told you about. He's a good friend of mine."

"Hello Clay, it's a pleasure to meet you."

"Thank you Mrs King, and the pleasure's all mine." I hadn't told my mother about Clay because I knew she would try and convince me to stay in Atlanta if she even thought I had a chance at happiness, but she didn't blow my cover...yet.

"Lane, why didn't you tell me Clay was coming? It was rude of us not to be here to greet him." Clay answered before I could even open my mouth; he knew I was still too stunned by his presence.

"No, Mrs King. Lane wasn't aware that I was coming. I thought I'd surprise her the way she surprised y'all." I could finally formulate a sentence.

"And what a terrific surprise it is, how did you know where my parents lived?"

"I got in touch with Charmine yesterday. She thought this surprise would be the spirit lifter you needed."

"But how did you get Char's number?"

"I hired a private detective," he jokes, "it was on my caller ID from the weekend you called her from my house."

"Ooh, you would make a good detective. That's probably why she was trying to get up with me."

"I'm glad she didn't, I enjoyed seeing your expression." My mother excused herself and hinted for my dad and aunt to follow so that Clay and I could talk. When they exited the room, I kissed him the way my body had yearned to kiss him since I've been gone. I asked him what really made him come. He joked saying that I was teasing him with the phone sex and he had to come feel some real flesh. I playfully slapped his shoulder.

"No Lane for real; I just heard it in your voice, you sounded like you wanted me here with you but wouldn't ask."

"You're right, how did you figure that out?"

"As I told you so many times before, I'm in the business of paying attention, and especially to those I care about." I gave him another warm kiss, which made me forget I was standing in the middle of my parents living room. My Aunt Bernice's laugh brought us back into the present. I asked him when he was going back, he told me he had to leave tonight he just wanted to check in with me and my folks and make sure all were good. The words leaving tonight made me wince. I didn't want him to go, but I knew he couldn't stay. I tried to tell him about my visit with Dre but he stopped and apprized me that this visit was about me. He added that as long as I was satisfied with the end result, he felt good just knowing that I handled my business, so I left it like that.

The caterers showed up before time, and did an excellent job with the food, and set up. I was glad the caterers were on point, as my dad's guests started arriving promptly at 7pm that night. I must admit, it felt as through Prince made his song just for this occasion, because we sure partied like it was 1999. The Grants; Charmine's parents came as promised and asked me to divulge any information I had on Anthony. I told them the only thing I knew about him thus far was that he was in love with their daughter. That seemed to satisfy Mrs Grant, but on the other hand, Mr Grant was going to need a little longer getting use to the fact that Anthony was white. I felt like Cinderella watching the clock knowing that Clay would have to leave me soon. I watched how Beverly and a few others of my cousins hovered in a corner of my parent's living room like buzzards, as they watched Clay like a hawk. I should be used to it by now. each time we went out; we got the same reaction. Why should I expect my cousins to be any different?

Clay pulled me into my room and told me he has to prepare to leave and reminds me that a car will be at Hartsfield on Sunday morning to bring me straight to his house. I thought that was perfect, I could break the news to him then. I clung to him so tightly, as he told me that I'll be alright, it's not like I'm not going to see him anymore. My tears are now flowing freely, I didn't know how to respond to what he just said. "Don't cry baby. Just look forward to Sunday; it's only two more days." He wiped my tears and kissed me on my neck. He re-joined my dad and his guests to thank them and said his good byes. My mother and I walked him to the door. When she told him how nice it was to meet him and hopefully this won't be their last meeting, he assured my mother that is wasn't. She left us to have our last few private moments. Clay took that time to remind me that I'm coming directly to his house and that my surprise would take place on Friday, so to try and cheer up. A kiss, and a slap on my ass later, Clay is headed back to Atlanta.

Relay-tionships

Chapter Thirteen

The party was a success. After singing happy birthday to my dad and he cut his cake, my aunts helped us pack the leftover food. Mostly in their bags to take home, which was fine because there would be no way my parents could have finished it all. After the last guest said their thank-yous and goodnights my mother wanted to know why I hadn't told her about Clay as I told him I did.

"I just didn't feel the time was right."

"When were you planning to tell me about him; every time you looked at me and regretted you moved here, and resented me in the process?"

"No ma and you know that wouldn't be the case. Ma look; it has been a beautiful, but tiring day. Can we not talk about this tonight?"

"Okay, you're right and this will be all I'll say for tonight. I know you said you two just met, but he's in love with you... and you with him. Your dad and I knew each only for nine months before we got married and that was over forty years ago. Good night baby sleep well." My dad said that had to be the best party he has ever had. He kissed me goodnight and thanked me again for such a memorable party as he chuckled all the way to his bedroom, catching a flashback on Uncle Snuck's non-dance moves. I called Char before I hit the bed for the night.

"What's up lady?"

"What's up with you?"

"Tell me everything, did you pee your pants when you saw Clay?"

"Hell yeah, thanks for trying to warn me. I tried calling you back hundreds of times but your phone was either going to voicemail or switched off."

"Oh yeah about that…I wasn't calling you about Clay's surprise visit, I wanted you to abort the visit you had with Dre. I had the chance to talk Clay in length and I felt it would be futile to waste your time visiting him. You know what, Clay is a good guy and he adores you already. The reason I wasn't taking your calls was because I knew I would have let the cat out of the bag if I had spoken to you and Clay's name came up."

"Girl, it's almost like you're psychic when it comes to Dre, and boy I hate you didn't reach me before I visited with that asshole."

"What has he done now?"

"Nothing worth talking about now, I'll catch you up when I get home. You know your parents had me hemmed up asking about Anthony."

"What did you tell them?"

"The truth. That you two love each other and nothing was going to interfere with that. I threw that in for your dad sake, because Anthony has his work cut out for him to win your dad over."

"I know and he will, he has three months to do it. We set a date for the 7th of May." Charmine went on to tell me how talented Faizon is and how she can't wait to wear her dress.

The day before I was headed back to Atlanta, I watched my dad get dressed in his golfer's clothes and head to the golf course with some of his buddies. My mom and I stayed home and chilled out rehashing my dad's party. Every time she touched on the subject of Clay and me I changed the subject. She didn't realize how difficult it was for me... or did she. I helped my mother prepare a calendar with all of her doctor's appointments and dates she would go in for her chemotherapy. I asked her was she afraid, she told me that she was at first, but one of her favorite scriptures helped her out tremendously and that was "Fear not, for I AM always with you." I admired her courage, because I know I would have been a basket-case.

With dad being out with his buddies most of the day, I took advantage of being a little girl again. I cuddled in bed with my mother to watch our favorite Betty Davis and Joan Crawford movies in black in white. When I felt my mother doze off, I got up and started packing. I was getting anxious to get home and talk to Clay and make the necessary preparations to come back to Brooklyn.

That night I tossed and turned until I realized there was no way I was going to get any sleep, and I might as well get up. The night was still and silent except for the occasional grunts that escaped my dad's body as he slept. Soon the sun peeked from the night and I sat at the kitchen table to have a cup of coffee. I heard my mother waking my dad, reminding him that I was leaving this morning. They both emerged from their room with the long face.

"Good morning, my king and queen, tea is served." I said to them, watching them put on fake smiles to keep our spirits up. I knew it would be like this that's why I booked the earliest departure flight available. I told them to just give me a month and I would be back for good, so it was no need for the long faces. My mother thanked me for such a pleasant trip and all of the help with my dad's party. They both sent their love to Clay, Faizon and Charmine. The taxi blew his horn and my dad attempted to grab my bags to help me to the door, but I stopped him because I wanted to prevent any last minute tactic he may use to interfere with my plans. I kissed them both goodbye at the door and told them I will call them as soon as I landed. The trip back to Atlanta seemed like an eternity. As soon as we landed, I hustled to get to baggage claims to collect my luggage. My one constellation was that Clay's driver would be there to take me directly to him. I had no time to waste. I looked to my left and as promised; I see a man holding a sign with, "King" posted on a white board, waiting for me to be taken to paradise. I called my parents first and Clay second. He said he couldn't wait to see me and he would leave the door unlocked and for me to just come in.

Sundays are traffic free in the morning; therefore, we arrived at Clay's in no time at all. I walked up the few cobblestone steps to Clay's house and opened the unlocked door, no sign of Clay. I called out to him and he yelled out for me to meet him upstairs. I ran upstairs to find Clay standing in his bedroom, bare chested with just his long black silk pj's. Wordless, Clay took me into his bathroom where he has prepared me a bath; lined with white rose petals and a tray of the reddest strawberries dipped in chocolate I have ever seen, topped with two glasses of Champagne to welcome me home. I can't wait to see what else he's arranged in honor of my home coming. Still hushed, he undressed me and helped me slip into the bath. He kneeled as he fed me the strawberries and we sipped on champagne. His silence was so intense that, that in itself was a turn on, but his eyes spoke to me and I understood everything he said. Lovingly he sponged my body, slowly massaging my breasts with his thick fingers. It amazed me how his strong hands felt, so sensuous as he nestled his fingers inside me, slowly and gently, in and out. I threw my leg over the side of the bath, so he can intrude me even deeper.

With my eyes closed and my body in euphoria, I now needed to feel his body pressed against mine. I took his fingers from inside me and placed them in my mouth and with the warm wetness of my other hand, I stroked his manhood. Clay took my wet body and carried me to his bed where he made love to me with such intense passion, I felt him erupt inside me. As we laid in each other's arms, I thought of how I would tell him I was moving back home. Now is not the time but soon…soon. We were drained after spending most of the day in bed making love, so Clay had our food delivered. Waiting on our food, I called Char and Faizon to let them know I was back in Atlanta. Clay tried his hardest to persuade me to spend the night, but I reminded him I had work and I had a lot of catching up to do after being off for a week. After we ate, I asked him to take me home. He continued to protest but I wouldn't waiver, so he gave in and drove me home.

I almost forgot about the surprise Clay had for me, until he asked me was I serious about liking hip-hop. I convinced him I was a hip-hop fanatic by answering all of his hip hop trivia correctly. I was really curious now, but the only hint he gave me was that I would thank him. Was he planning to put me in one of his videos? I shook that idea out of my head; I knew I was a tad bit too old to be a video vixen.

Clay called me on Tuesday with another surprise in store for me; he wanted me to meet his Treasured Trio. Oh boy this was major; he wanted me to meet his mother and big ma. I knew I had to tell him and it had to be before I met the three most important women in his world. I desperately wanted to meet all of them, but I did not want to allow myself to get any closer knowing what I was preparing to do. I called Char for advice and she voted for me to be totally honest; after all, he would have to understand my reason. After I spoke to Char, I felt I did need to be fair to him. I called while he was still at work hoping that would deter him from asking me a slew of questions, but I quickly learned that didn't help.

"What's up baby, what ya doing?"

"What's up with you?"

"I'm discussing a treatment for a video we're about to shoot, what's going on?"

"Clay, you know I think the world of you... but I don't think this is the right time for me to meet your mother."

"Hold up!" I heard him ask his folks to clear his office. When he came back to me, his voice was stern. "What do you mean, now is not the right time. What's going on Lane?"

"Nothing is going on; I just don't think that the time is right."

"Here you go with that bullshit again; I told you I can live without. What happened to you would be straightforward from here on in and no more games! Do you remember you said that to me Lane?" I felt horrible, I do remember my words to him and he deserved the truth. I didn't plan (for me) to tell him this over the phone but I knew him well enough now, that if I don't tell him something; it's over. Timorous, I began to speak. "Clay, I have something to tell you, which I tried since

I've been back from my parents." I hesitated before I continued and Clay makes it clear his patience is running thin.

"What have you tried to tell me?"

"Clay…I'm moving back to N.Y."

"You're doing what?"

"I'm moving back home."

"Oh I get it; your visit with Dre must have went better than what you let on. It's like that? Dude got you on lock!" I didn't know how to respond to that but I wanted him to know the truth but not over the phone.

"Clay, it's not what you think. Please believe me, my move back home has nothing to do with Dre, I swear."

"Then what Lane? I find myself thinking about you all the time and I thought we were getting closer."

"I do too and we are. I don't want to talk about why over the phone, it's difficult enough."

"All right, I'm leaving the office now. I'll meet you at your house, so be there." I understood his anger, I should have told him by now. I had a bad habit of handling my affairs with avoidance, like sneaking my resignation letter on Mr Wyatt's desk while he was out to lunch, but Clay was not having it. When I got home he was already parked in my driveway. He sat in the car until I'm out of my car and has opened the door. I can see his face, but he just has a dead stare in his eyes. He finally came in and without any rhetoric, stood by my front door a quick escape route if he's not satisfied with my answer. Point blank, he asked me what the hell is going on.

I sat on my sofa and stared up into his eyes searching for the tenderness that I so needed from him, while I poured my heart out to him. "Clay, my move has nothing to do with Dre. I told you and I meant it when I said we are through. It's my mother

Clay she needs me." He unfolds his arms and his face softens as I continue. "While I was home we found out that my mother's cancer has returned and has spread throughout her body." Clay broad shoulders have rounded and he placed a half-open fist to his lips. His body language indicated he wished he could take back every accusatory word he spat at me.

He came over to sit next to me and I felt his tenderness has returned, as he cradled me in his arms. He apologized profusely for his thoughtlessness. "Lane I'm so sorry to hear that. Why didn't you tell me sooner? I would have never spoken to you like that. Times like these I always want to be there for you." As he cradled me, I cried but honestly, I didn't know why. Were my tears for my mother or for me having to leave Clay? That night he stayed with me just to talk. With him being a businessman, he sat me down with pen and paper with all of the different options that were available to me. He was hoping that I might have overlooked something, some way to avoid me moving back home. When he saw that I wasn't going to budge from my stance, he resigned to the fact, he had to accept my decision.

"Lane, let me ask you something. What do you feel about us?"

"What do you mean?"

"Just what I said, what do you feel about us?"

"Clay, I love being with you. From the first day I saw you over the sky cam you had me, and now that I'm with you... I want you even more and to think that I leaving you... I'm devastated."

"Me too. I don't think I ever told you this but, when I first saw you from behind it was pure lust, until you turned to me. Your eyes and lips fucked me up. I told my boy that night at the game, I had to have you and now that I know Lane;

the person. I am not willing to give you up, we'll make this shit work."

"But how Clay, long distance relationships aren't long lived."

"You act like you're moving to Siberia; you'll still be in the same time zone." Finally, we had something to laugh about. I thought about what my mother said, I couldn't speak for Clay, but I knew I was in love.

"With the news of your moms are you up to going out on Friday?"

"Yes, so don't try and get out of it. I waited almost two weeks for it, so yeah I want it."

"In that case, I'll be here at eight to pick you up."

"Good, I can't wait." I answered with a flirtatious feistiness. Tonight was the first time we laid in each other arms flesh to flesh and just slept.

Chapter Fourteen

The next morning I over-slept, and I had to leave Clay still in my bed. God, I envied him being able to come and go as he pleased; now that was the true meaning of being free. I knew he worked hard because he was successful, but he sure made it look so easy. I wasn't in the bank a half hour before Mr Wyatt called me into his office, no doubt to talk about my resignation. Sure enough, I walked in and he is holding my letter in his hands with a look of surprise on his face.

"Lane would you like to explain."

"Of course Mr Wyatt. I know my explanation was vague in my letter, and that's because it's so personal. My mother is sick and I need to be there for her plain and simple."

"I'm terribly sorry to hear that. I did notice you have been a bit distracted since you've come back. Lane I am saddened that we are losing one of our brightest stars, but believe me, I do understand. You will be missed and if there is anything I can do please let me know. Will you continue to work? because if you do, I will personally call some people at Salomon and r."

Mr Wyatt, but I haven't thought that far, but
me take this time to say it has been a pleasure
rking with you, and thank you very much for
understanding."

"You're welcome Lane, just let me know if you change your
mind about the phone calls."

"I will." I left his office and breathed a sigh of relief,
knowing that I wouldn't have a problem finding a job, if and
when I decided to go back to work. I knew Niecy would be
jam-packed Friday, so I made an appointment to get my hair
done on Thursday for my big night out with Clay on Friday.
Clay and I talked on the phone, since he was so busy with his
new artists and wanting to get this video just right, but he told
me to make sure I was ready by eight when he picked me up. I
knew my time with Clay was getting short and I wanted to
unleash all my inhibitions to make it a night he would not
soon forget. That night I dreamed of all the things I wanted to
perform on Clay. I woke up still remembering most of them,
my body still in trembles.

I talked to my mother and discovered she was still feeling
weak and in excruciating pain. My dad took the phone and
told me that the doctor wrote her a prescription to ease the
pain, and informed me that her first treatment was scheduled
for Friday morning. I told my dad I was glad to hear that she
had something to alleviate her pain, and that Char and I would
be there next weekend to look at some apartments for me, once
I moved back home. Char wanted to see my mother and her
parents. She made it a point that she wanted to talk to her dad
before he traveled to Atlanta for the wedding. She felt her
mother would be welcoming to Anthony, but couldn't be that
abiding for her dad's response. At lunchtime Owen, the bank

security officer informed me, that I have a visitor. I knew it wasn't Clay, as he was on location shooting his treatment and I just got off the phone with Char. I told Owen thank you, and walked up front. I gasped in delight at the one and only Black Barbie. Faizon was in full effect and standing in the lobby of the bank, looking absolutely stunning in one of her own designs and a Malene Birger cape. Who would have ever thought that just barely a month ago, she was near death.

"Hello sweetie." She grinned from ear to ear as she greeted me.

"Look at you, you look fantastic! What are you doing here?"

"I've come to take you to lunch."

"Shit perfect timing because I'm starving. I ran back to my office long enough to grab my bag and met Faizon out front. We were both in the mood for Mexican and stopped at a restaurant on Piedmont. Faizon told me she wanted to show me her newest designs and brought her pad into the restaurant. We ordered our food, and as we wait (for our food), I looked through her design pad. She showed me Char's wedding dress, along with the dress she'd wear at the reception and swatches of the materials she'd be using. She is extremely gifted and Darnell tried to cheat the world by taking her away, but God put a monkey wrench in his plan. We talked a bit about her twinges of sadness when she thought about the baby, and her outright disgust for Darnell. She mentioned how the prosecutor promised her, and her parents he would seek the max which was twenty- five to life without the possibility of parole. That made me feel just about as good as seeing Faizon up and about.

After our incredible lunch and talk, I headed back to the bank to finish work on time. I had a hair appointment in Stone Mountain that I wasn't going to miss. By the time my hair was picture perfect and I got home, it was after nine and all I wanted to do was shower and hit the bed. Clay gave me his nightly call and told me that the shoot went better than he expected and asked me about my day.

"Clay you will never guess who took me to lunch today?"

"Umm, I know it wasn't Char because that wouldn't excite you like this, so it had to be Faizon."

"Exactly, and she looked amazing. Her body and mind strong, she even showed me the dresses for Char's wedding day."

"That's good to hear baby, I'm glad that made your day." Trying to get a feel of where he would be taking me tomorrow, I asked him what I should wear. He's been around me long enough now to know when I was trying to play him out. And gave me a smug answer.

"Baby, you could wear a Kroger bag and you'll still be fine. Listen baby, I had a long day and I'm tired as hell, I will see you tomorrow. I love you Lane, goodnight"

"I love you too, see you tomorrow." We hung up and it hit me like a sledgehammer. We had just said I love you to each other. I wondered was he sitting on his bed realizing what he just said. For me it flowed so natural, it felt good. Fuck worrying about if I said it too soon, I'm in love. That night while I slept; I had an indescribable sensation that sat me straight up, but I couldn't put my finger on it, so I dismissed it and forced myself to go back to sleep. Have Fridays have now became my Mondays. I knew I would have to use everything I learned in college about time management today. I already knew what I'd be wearing. What I needed was a new fuck me negligee for tonight when Clay and I got back to my house. Clay called me while I was on my way to work and told me to have a good day, and how bad he needed to see me tonight. I wanted to address the issue of us saying I love you to each other, but I didn't want to make a big deal out of it. What if he hadn't meant to say it, how would I handle that. I told him to enjoy his day too and I would see him tonight at eight. I got through my day just fine and I owed it all to Professor Leonard for teaching the art of time management. I made a stop at Dial Sun and got my eye- brows waxed and headed to Phelps Plaza for that special little pick me up for Clay.

I checked the time, and realized I had no time to dilly-dally. Without further delay, I pointed my car towards home. By the time I reached home, I knew my mother should have been home from her treatment by now also. I called my parents to check on my mother before I left for the night. Not that I wanted to remember, but I couldn't forget how harsh the chemo treatments were for my mother in the past. I remembered that the chemo would have my mother's body in pain and as before, would have her feeling extremely poorly. I just hoped, this time around, it wouldn't be as severe.

"Hi there ma, how did everything go today?"

"Not so good. Between the nausea and the coughing, I'm pooped, but don't worry about me because you know these are the side effects."

"I know mommy. I can't help but to worry about you and I hate I can't do anything to make you feel better."

"I won't say that. Your dad brought a smile to my face when he told me you will be here next weekend visiting with Char."

"Yeah, she is flying with me this time. She really wants to see you."

"That's sweet; it will be nice to see her too. Her mother called me yesterday to see how I was feeling and to tell me what a nice time they had at your dad's birthday party."

"That was sweet and you sound exhausted, so I will call you when I get in tonight if it's not too late. Clay is taking me on a surprise date tonight and guess what? He told me he loved me last night. I had to laugh thinking about what you told me last week about you and daddy. Ma… let me ask you this, how can you tell Clay's in love with me?"

"I saw it in his eyes when you walked in the room." I laughed at her answer, because I'm a firm believer that the eyes don't lie and now I had my mother to confirm it. I still had a funny feeling, but I just chalked it up to being in love. "Baby, I may not tell you this enough but I want you to know that I love you so much. You've made me and your dad, extremely proud of you and if I don't talk to you tomorrow, please know that you mean the world to me."

"Well it sure wasn't hard with parents like you and daddy. Get some rest and of course I'll talk to you tomorrow. I love you mommy, kiss daddy for me." After me and my mom hung up, I laid my night out like a road map in my mind. When Clay brings me home, I'll bring him pleasure, he could only wish for. I amused myself with the x-ratedness that engorged my mind and finished with my preparations before he reached my house. I looked in my mirror, and hoped we even make it to our planned destination; as good as I looked tonight. I wanted to get that jaw dropping response from Clay tonight, and I believe I have achieved that. Precisely at eight, Clay rings my bell and when I opened the door, before he fully entered, he stopped dead in his tracks and looked at me. Good, just the reaction I wanted.

Clay looked impressive as well, he always had his shit together and tonight was no different, well one slight difference; he had a little more ice than he normally wore out. He told me if we wanted to be on time, we had better leave now, but not before he took the opportunity to tell me how exceptional he thought I looked and how he couldn't wait to get me back home. That brought us both to laughter, knowing full well what that meant. Clay helped me with my coat and he locked up behind us. He chauffeured me into his car and got in a quick kiss and we were on our way.

"Alright Mister, I think it is safe to tell me where you are taking me."

"You're a smart woman, I thought you have figured it out by now. I've been giving you little clues here and there."

"What clues!? You asked me a few questions about hip-hop, and told me to remember what we talked about on our first date. The only thing I've come up with is that you want me in one of your videos." He found that to be hysterically humorous.

"Okay... it's not that funny." I replied, laughing now about as hard as he is.

"I know, I know, I just wondered out of all things you could have guessed, why you thought that; although you are fine enough to be in my video."

"I don't know. I just want to know."

"Since you can't seem to figure it out, I'll tell you this much, we're almost there." I could see we're headed to Philips Arena where we first met. I knew it wasn't a basketball game tonight, but as we got closer; I saw it was a concert there, but who was it. Clay told me that as part of my surprise, I had to be blindfolded. At first, I flat out refused, but I gave in when I saw how much trouble he went to, so at the next light Clay placed a silk scarf to cover my eyes. He told me to trust him and relax, and I did just that. The noise was a clear indication that we had arrived at the Philips. I allowed Clay to guide me up stairs and on elevators; I could hear a male group singing I just couldn't make out who they were yet. I was being lead down what I believed to be a corridor lined with people.

I heard voices speaking to Clay, and one guy even asked Clay could he leave him his demo. Clay told him tonight was not a good time but to drop it off by his office. With the excitement, I heard in the guy's voice, I wouldn't have been surprised if he had taken it to Clay's office tonight. Suddenly Clay stopped and I heard him knock on a door. The door was pulled open and Clay was still playing the role of my eyes. We walked in, Clay hands still firmly clutched my waist, I heard a voice greet Clay by asking him "what was up." I heard the slapping of hands, so it was apparent that Clay knew the individual and oddly enough, the male that was speaking to Clay, sounded familiar. Clay told the male voice, thanks for making this happen and asked me was I ready to be unveiled. Painfully anxious, I panted yes. When Clay pulled the scarf from my eyes, my vision was still blurred from having the scarf on for that length of time.

When my eyes was in full focus, I stood in perfect shock to discover that, I was standing in Busta Rhymes dressing room, in front of Busta himself. Stiff as a three-month old frozen pork chop in the deep freezer, I stood there. I didn't know what to say, or how to react. I looked at Clay in amazement and then it all came back to me. On our first date. I told him how I'd love to meet Busta Rhymes, and tonight, he had made that dream come true. Clay told Busta the story of our first date and what a huge fan I am of his. I had been silent long enough and found the words to tell Busta for myself, what a fan I've been of his since Leaders of the New School. He thanked me, signed an autograph, and invited us to his after party. I can't deny that I love Busta, but I was glad to hear that

Clay declined on his offer. I had our own after party planned for us back at the house, but that didn't stop us from watching Busta-bust perform from backstage. Busta performed on stage like only he can, I felt like I was in my school days again, as I rapped right along with him on every one of his tracks. What Clay had just done for me was enormous, I felt great and I will never forget it!

I turned to Clay with such adoration, I knew this was the man that could make my dreams come true. I no longer doubted if our relationship would work with me living in New York. I tried my best to restrain my gratitude for him in public but I just couldn't hold back any longer. I kissed Clay with such fervor, he wanted to leave the arena and head home, before the concert even concluded. I eagerly obliged, visualizing what would await him at home, as Clay and I speed walked to his Escalade. I couldn't wait until we pulled onto Amelis Road. I leaned into Clay and nibbled at his ear and softly kissed on his neck. I deliberately panted in his ears because I discovered he liked that.

I told Clay I had to show him how appreciative I was of him going to all that trouble for me to meet Busta and it was now his turn for the blindfold. I used the very same scarf, covered his beautiful eyes, and carefully walked his tall lean body into the house. I asked him did he want a drink before I started my show. Still blindfolded he accepted and I poured him a glass of Hennessey. I set the mood and played some Maxwell softly in background and lead Clay into a candlelit bathroom. I started to undress him slowly and seductively, giving attention to his body with my tongue until he was in only his skin. I told Clay that he must keep the blindfold on until I give him permission to take it off. He gave me a sexy smirk, but obliged me, as he sat comfortably in my Queen Anne lounge chair, I positioned in front of my shower as the show was about to begin. I stood behind Clay as I undressed, allowing my breasts to brush against his naked skin while I prepared for our show. With my attire, now matching Clay's, I walked to turn on my huge head shower. When I asked Clay to reveal his eyes, he found me in my shower with black stilettos and the water cascading my naked body. Clay sat back as deep as my chair would allow him; one hand hung over my chair as his other hand smoothed out his own goatee.

I lathered my body with Lavender and Jasmine while masturbating myself. Through my seduction, I watched Clay as he watched me, and although he sat patiently, his manhood wasn't as disciplined. Through the warm water, that hit my body, I watched his manhood extend to its full potential. Clay watched me intensely, as my hands caressed my own breasts and placed one in my mouth. I slid my fingers down my flat stomach to enter my pussy as the soapy lather slid into the bottom of my stilettos. I held my head back and permitted the water to run to through my hair. While I continued to pleasure myself, I heard the deep moans of Clay wanting desperately to join me. He didn't wait much longer for an invitation, as he accompanied me in the water. Heaving, he took my breasts in his mouth while the water (now) enveloped the both of us. With a fierce passion, he turned my body towards the wall of my shower, and entered me from behind. With each impassioned thrust, Clay held onto me tighter until I screamed in delight and Clay and I climaxed together. Our bodies drained, Clay carried me to my bed, where Clay rested his head on my breasts, and I rubbed his smooth goatee. I wanted to speak, but I just didn't have the strength.

"Clay, I want you to know that you astounded me tonight. No man has ever gone to such great lengths to make me feel this way."

"I find that a problem. You shouldn't have to feel like your man is going out of his way or feel your happiness is a chore. It should be as natural as the love he has for you, and I love you Lane." His brown eyed gaze, pierced through my body and I told him I loved him too. So it wasn't a fluke last night, his I love you was intentional. He continued to lay his head on my chest, while I dreamed about our future together. My phone rang awakened us. Clay who was laying closest to my phone peeked at caller id and announced it was Char. I wondered what she could possibly want at this time of morning. I asked Clay to answer the phone while I ran into the bathroom.

I could hear Clay telling Char I had to use the bathroom. They continued to speak, but Clay's voice was almost in a hushed whisper. I washed my hands quickly, and re-entered my bedroom to take Char's call. Clay stood by the bed still clutching the phone in his hands. I could tell from where I was standing that his face was numb, and the closer he got, the more numbed he looked. "What's the matter Clay, what did Char want at this time of morning?" His mouth was agape but he couldn't speak, I attempted to grab the phone from him to hit redial and find out for myself, what had Clay so aphonic. Clay prevented me from calling Char back. He took the phone from my hands and threw it on my bed, he told me that Charmine was on her way over at my dad's request. Clay grabbed me by both my hands and attempted to sit me on my bed. I was confused by what Clay was telling me, my heart started to race and my face contorted, I could see the words leave his mouth, but I couldn't believe what I was hearing. It sounded like he said my mother was gone. Suddenly I was surrounded by the darkest blackness, which was all around me, and a chilling shrill, escaped my body, which weakened me until I could no longer stand. I didn't know why now, my mind was flooded with all the relationships, which have meant so much to me in the past and the relationships I would come to cherish in the future. How could this be happening? I am now faced with the loss of my most precious relationship.

The End?